UNDER PRESSURE

UNDER PRESSURE

By Mr. D

Published by
MIDNIGHT EXPRESS BOOKS

UNDER PRESSURE

ISBN-10: 098576869X
ISBN-13: 978-0-9857686-9-0

Cover art by Aldi Caban

Disclaimer: This is a work of fiction. All characters are totally from the imagination of the author and depict no persons, living or dead; any similarity is totally coincidental.

Published by
MIDNIGHT EXPRESS BOOKS
POBox 69
Berryville AR 72616
(870) 210-3772
MEBooks1@yahoo.com

This one is dedicated to my older brother, Stanley, who died from a drug overdose twenty-five days before he turned twenty-five, before he had learned how to live.

Another deserving of praise is my best ally, unpaid secretary, friend, and sister, whom I'll call Gail the Great for this project. She's the greatest!

Prelude

Wind howled between the walls and razor wire at the federal penitentiary in Leavenworth, Kansas, as he sat contemplating how to eliminate the problem, Jake Stephens. A winter storm pounded the plains with layers of white powder; a beautiful sight for those with sleds, skis, and snowmobiles, but to Stan Mason it was just another dreary day in the pen. He sipped bitter-black coffee from a clear plastic coffee mug, while he stared at puke-green walls. Someone shouted something inaudible that interrupted his thoughts. A gun would be great, one shot to the head and no more Jake. A gun wasn't an option: a shank was the best thing available.

PART I

CHAPTER 1 – The Shank

"Hey, Bobby, come here," he yelled. Bobby lived two cells down the tier. It was quieter than normal. Most of his fellow prisoners laid in their beds to stay warm, covered with green or gray Army blankets. Sound travelled easily because people weren't out of bed making noise.

"Okay. Give me a few seconds."

Over the last few years, they had developed a trust for each other, and knew each would hold their ground during conflict--a rare trait amongst the typical modern-day prisoners.

A few seconds later, Bobby stepped to the door. "Good morning," he said.

Stan did not have a cellmate. He motioned him to come in and then spoke low to avoid being heard by his neighbors. "I need to get strapped-up to go take care of that punk." He sat on the bed in gray sweat pants and nursed a cup of java. Bobby ducked to enter the cell. Stan sipped his coffee and peeked over the mug and waited for a response.

Bobby used the "Throne" in the rear of the cell as a seat. He stared for a moment, raised his eyebrows, and leaned forward to rest his elbows on his knees.

"What's up?" he said. Then he put his hands together and made an arch with two fingers, placed them across his thin lips.

"He's putting pressure on Terry to have Wendy to bring in some tar," he said. Then he sipped some java and set the cup on the edge of the bed. "Terry's all for it, but, he knows I don't want him putting her in that kind of a position, and I'll be damned if I'll let him. What if she got caught?"

"Shouldn't that be their business?"

"Hell, no, Terry's sick and will do anything for his next fix. That's his business. Wendy's my sister and that makes it my business." he said. He stood, set the coffee mug on the battleship gray storage locker and frowned. "She's still young and deserves more in life than someone like that."

"No doubt," Bobby said. "She deserves much better."

"I can't stand by and let anyone do something that might get her thrown in one of these hell-holes. Understand?" His face was flushed, eyebrows arched, and his forehead wrinkled. He gritted his teeth and the muscles in his angular jaw flexed, stuck out on the sides. After a second he relaxed his jaw and grabbed the coffee mug, held it, rubbed his thumb across the ridges on its handle. "I'm not going to let it happen," he said. "I'm sorry, man. I can't do it."

Bobby stood and leaned against the wall with his broad back. Stan put the cup on the locker and then raised the corner of his mattress, where he had hidden a flattened roll of duct tape. He handed the tape to Bobby and then got six GQ magazines from his locker and threw them on the bed. Then he reached under the locker for an eight-inch piece of sharpened stainless steel he had stashed. Bobby snorted like a Brahman bull and wrinkled his nose. Stan glanced at him and waited two seconds for the lecture he knew was coming.

"That's cool, but how will she feel when she finds out that you killed Jake over her and Terry's business? You haven't even given her a chance to decide on it. She may not do it. Have you thought about that?"

"Not really," he said, then he looked out the cell-door window.

"How's she going to feel when you get caught and spend the rest of your life in here with me?"

Stan knew Bobby was serving life without parole for a murder on military property at Fort Bragg, North Carolina, and that he was scheduled to die in prison.

"I don't know, man," he said as he looked at the floor. "I ain't thought about it that way." He grabbed the piece of steel, handed Bobby the pointed end to hold. Then he reached into his sweat pants pocket and pulled out a strip of camo green duck cloth he'd stolen from the textile plant where he worked making military products. From his other pocket, he took a boot lace for tying the cloth to the handle. Before he began wrapping the cloth around the blunt end of the shank, he glanced up at Bobby, who towered a foot above his six-foot-frame. Bobby shook his head and tightened his lips until they almost disappeared. Stan knew he was disappointed in him for what he was doing.

"Bro, I know you're right. That's something to consider, but I don't know of any other way to handle it."

"Why not forget it and let Wendy make her own choice. You're not her daddy, pal."

Stan gritted his teeth and would have punched anyone else for such a comment, but he loved Bobby as much as he would his own brother. He didn't want him to be mad at him, and sure didn't want to tangle with someone big enough to wrestle a grizzly bear and win, so he took a deep breath. "I got to go, man," he said. "Look down the tier for me, all right. I ain't gonna change my mind."

Bobby ducked and walked out on the tier, leaned against the dull yellow rail for a minute, and then eased back into the cell. "Everything's cool," he said.

Stan made a large loop with part of the boot lace that he tied to the handle before securing it with the duct tape. "It's just a bad situation I'm caught up in."

"You know, some choices are permanent and have long-lasting consequences. If you take someone's life, well, it's not something you can give back or do over. Just think about it before doing something you'll regret later."

"I hear what you're saying." He wished he would shut up.

Bobby moved closer to a bowl of assorted candies on the locker, snatched a lemon sour and popped it into his mouth. "Listen to me. Don't you know I wish I'd never gotten drunk and blacked out before I killed that man? I've wished a million times that I could take back what I did, but I can't. It's not easy living with the knowledge that they'll carry me out in a box, but that's not what bothers me. It's killing the man, I regret. I don't want to see you in the same position, bro, which is why I'm taking the time to talk to you. You're my partner. You know that."

"All right. That's good," Stan said. He took the shank and slid the loop over his hand to check the fit. "Man, that's deep, but I'm not trying to hear it. I've got it in my mind to take care of it the best way I know how. There's no other way to stop them from ruining her life, other than killing Terry to put the poor bastard out of his misery, but I prefer taking Jake out. I can't stand the punk!"

Bobby shook his head. "Get real, pal."

"Man, Jake ain't no good. He raped and robbed a lady at some National park, or something like that. That's why he's doing time. He's not worth killing, but I'm killing him anyway," he said. Then he looked down at the blade and squeezed its handle as he stroked the edge with his other hand. He clinched his jaw when he saw Bobby smirking, as if the situation was funny.

"So, big man, let me get this straight. Now it's up to you to clean up the world by disposing of all its undesirables, huh? Don't you think that's God's job?"

Stan fumed. Bombarded by thoughts of comprising a defensive comeback and finding none, he started taping the magazines together in sets of two. He placed the first two against his chest. "Here, man, tape these to me." He struggled with what Bobby had said, knowing he was right, but not wanting to let it go. The intelligent self said back out. The egotistical self won. "He's nothing but a predator that preys on the weak and wounded, and I'm going to do the world a good service by removing him from circulation."

Bobby taped two GQ's across Stan's chest, two across the back, and the last two across the abdominals. Afterward, Stan pulled on a gray sweat shirt, and then a jacket, while he contemplated his predicament. He tightened the shank's strap on his wrist to avoid dropping it. Two years ago, he had seen a man drop one, who reached down to pick it up and had gotten stabbed in the cervical, right below where the cranium connects to the spinal cord. He lay helpless afterward. He died before the hacks got him to the hospital. Bobby broke into his thoughts by speaking.

"What about Jessica and Jasmine? Don't you care for them?"

He opened his mouth, blinked his eyes, squinted, tried to speak but nothing came out. He stared at Bobby for a moment and then looked away, looked at

Jessica's letter on his locker. She was two-months-old when he was arrested, seven years ago. "Dammit, Bobby, I wish the hell you'd be quiet, man."

"Get over it, pal. You can't whip me and you're scared to stab me," Bobby said, and then laughed and slapped him on the back.

"You'll find out what I'll do if you don't leave me alone." Trying to act serious, he looked up and squinted again. He knew Bobby was joking and that neither would ever consider doing anything to cause injury to the other. He was also aware that Bobby knew he was talking trash, bluffing, because they played that way together. No one else played that way with them.

"Yeah, well, killer, answer my question."

"You know damn good and well that I love them," he said. Then he slid the blunt end of the shank up the sleeve of his jacket. "I never want to do anything to hurt them or Wendy, but I'm not going to sit around and wait for anyone to mess up my sister's life, when I know how to stop it." He paused for a moment while he positioned the point of the shank on his wrist by curling his hand. "I'm just in a bad situation," he said. Then he straightened his wrist to let the shank fall, which dropped farther than what he preferred, so he tightened the strap by pulling the loop. "Now, that's about right."

"Look, pal. You know I'm your partner and won't bullshit you. You need to think of another way to handle this. I know you hate Jake and I don't blame you. Don't let an idiot cause you to rot in here. Forget it and get your stupid ass out of prison."

"Man, fuck that," he said. He pushed the piece up his sleeve, while pondering what Bobby had said, hating every word because they had aroused something inside he didn't want to acknowledge existed: concern. Spending the rest of his life in prison wasn't something he wanted to do, but, ... He stared at him for a flash, kept the shank in place by bending his wrist, and then sipped java from the cup with his other hand.

Bobby leaned against the wall and shook his head.

"Don't give me that look, man. I know you're right, but I've got to do it anyway," he said. This time when he checked the reach, it fell right into position, with the handle level with his palm.

Adrenaline scorched Stan's veins when a guard rattled the doors by releasing and re-locking them with the electronic mechanism.

"Emergency count!" she yelled. "Lockdown in two minutes!"

The prisoners started to rush for their cells to avoid disciplinary action for disrupting an official count.

"Fuck, man. What the hell's this bullshit?" Stan said. "Hurry up and help me get these damn magazines off."

Bobby started yanking the strips of tape off as soon as Stan raised his jacket and sweat shirt. Stan worked on getting the strap loose enough to slide over his wrist so he could stash the shank under his pillow.

"You're snake-bit, pal," Bobby said, as he yanked off the last piece of tape holding everything together.

Stan wiped at the sweat gathering on his forehead. Bobby ducked his head and shot through the door when she shouted, "Closing them, gentlemen!" He barely made it back to his cell before she shut the doors with the electronic gang release/locking mechanism.

Moments later, two guards walked by Stan's cell counting; he had everything hidden from view. He stood facing the mirror in the back of his cell, combing his hair with a palm brush to avoid the risk of them noticing anything suspicious about the way he looked. His heart beat as if he had did a shot of meth or cocaine, pounding so hard that it felt like it was trying to break through the ribs to free itself from the chest cavity. One thing he didn't need was a shakedown by the guards.

After they had passed the cell counting, he sat on the edge of the bed for a few minutes waiting for the count to clear. He felt that it was an omen for them to decide to count when they did. If they'd counted five minutes later, he'd have already butchered Jake, or been in the process, with no chance of getting away with the murder. Maybe it was proof that Bobby was right, he should leave it alone and let it work itself out.

Sitting still became painful. Anxiety drove him to his feet. He got up and paced the tiny cell, three steps to the front, and three steps to the back. Fifteen minutes later, he laid down, propped his head up on the pillow with his fingers laced behind his head to help him think better. Within ten seconds, he was plotting on the future, reminiscing about lost days in Georgia.

Mr. D

CHAPTER 2 – The Oasis

Water flowed across the gray flat rocks that lined the river bed, smoothed by centuries of gentle pressure. Boulders larger than cars made miniature, white-crested, waterfalls in the Flint River. It was their favorite place. On most warm or sweltering summer days, Stan and Wendy jumped in the river to splash around and play like any other young children. On colder days, they'd sit on the bank: Stan eating Snickers; Wendy, M&Ms with peanuts, both drinking sodas as they watched the sun do its rhythmic dance on ripples of water.

Stan loved his baby sister and defended her against any of the bullies, never stopping to think about busting them in their mugs for disrespecting her. He did it on impulse. His sense of debt to her exceeded any threat of injury to himself. He literally owed her his life.

The Georgia sun showed no mercy in the August after he had turned ten. A light breeze relieved the misery for only a moment, while it slipped across the sweat. "Let's go, Sissy," he said.

"Where we goin'?" she asked.

"You know, where we always go; to the Oasis." In school he had learned about deserts and oasis'. A cartoon he enjoyed watching on television had an oasis in it. He loved the beauty of the oasis and imagined how it must feel to find one in the middle of a desert when dying of thirst. That's why he named his favorite spot on the river the Oasis. It made him feel refreshed. He was at peace while there, happy, pleased by all he could see and hear: birds chirping, the rustling of water slipping between boulders to caress the weeping willows growing on an island near the bank.

For most of his life, his parents had carried them to that spot to fish and play in the water. His dad mostly drank beer and fought with their mother, while him and Wendy ran through the woods, turning up logs and rocks to look for frogs and snakes. If not that, they'd go swimming. Both had learned to swim before they turned five: That's one good thing his dad had taught them.

Mr. D

The river ran a mile away from the back of their house. Two miles down the road it crossed under a bridge. The Oasis was somewhere between the two points. A rope hung from an oak branch that they used to swing out into the deeper part of the river. Twenty minutes after leaving the house that day, they had made it to the Oasis. Both had scratches on their little legs from rushing through the underbrush in their T-shirts and shorts. Stan hurried to the rope.

"Watch this, Sissy," he said. He ran and grabbed the rope and swung out over the river but waited too long to let go. He crashed into the water at an awkward angle, too close to the bank, with his shoulders and the back of his head striking the water first. His head hit the bottom.

Wendy watched, worried. Ten seconds later he hadn't resurfaced. Filled with fear, she dived in after him, and even though he outweighed her by twenty pounds, she managed to pull him to the edge of the river. "Stanley, ... wake ... up," she said, as she struggled to pull him up on the bank.

He coughed water, gasped for air. He opened his bloodshot eyes a second before he reached to rub a big bump on the back of his head. Wendy grabbed and hugged him.

He gazed into the distance for a few seconds before speaking. "What happened?"

"You didn't let go like you told me I should do."

"How did I get up here?"

"I jumped in and got you," she said. Her eyes were still filled with tears. "You didn't come up when you always do, so I jumped in and got you."

He never forgot that day. Wendy never mentioned it again. It was their secret.

Since their mom and dad were alcoholics and dope fiends, both children were usually left to care for themselves for most of the day. Neither Stan or Wendy minded because that's how they thought it went for all children like them. Besides, it was nice not having to go straight home from school; not having to go to bed early, and especially not having to stay at home and do homework.

10

Even when teachers sent home notes with them to complain, it didn't matter. Getting beat with a belt by their dad was the worst that happened. The beatings never ceased, it seemed.

He remembered one vicious beating when he was only six. The school was down the road. He snuck out of class to go play at the river. The principal of the school called to report him missing. His parents caught him walking down the road. "Get your ass in this car, boy," his dad had said.

As soon as they pulled in the garage and parked, his dad yanked him out of the car by the arm. "You're going to learn to mind, young man," he said, and then started pounding him with a thin, leather belt.

A minute later his Mom yelled, "Stop Darnell. His back's bleeding. You leave that boy alone, right now!" She had always defended him and Wendy.

"Bitch, you don't tell me how to raise my young'uns," he said. Then he turned and busted her lip with his fist. She fought back but gave up when he shoved her down and her head struck the concrete. Stan remembered the guilt he had carried for causing her to be beat, and the dreams he had had of being big enough to stop his dad from beating them. That had been his life: guilt. Years later, he laid on a hard mattress in a prison cell wondering how he had gotten there. Life as a child hadn't been so terrible, had it? He was beat a lot, of course, and had to watch his mother and sister be beat, but he had did all he could to stop it, hadn't he? So, why, why did he have to be there? He tried figuring out why his dad had been so mean. He couldn't. Maybe their granddad had beaten him the same way. What else could've made him that way? He didn't know.

After Wendy had saved him at the Oasis that day, he became overly-protective of her. He defended her against anyone, even their dad. If he trounced on her, he'd grab the belt or hit him to divert his attention. It worked. Their dad would forget Wendy and turn his fury toward him. He had been beat so much that he had grown immune to the pain and easily endured it: It only lasted a moment.

He and Wendy spent the next few years playing at the Oasis whenever possible. As they aged they still picnicked and partied down by the river, but never at the Oasis if anyone else was with them. It was their secret place.

CHAPTER 3 - Enough

Born in April, this was his twelfth Christmas. Outside it was more like spring than winter. No snow or ice, just an ample breeze to keep it cool. Bright rays of sunshine crested the oaks, pines, and maple trees in their front yard. He jumped out of bed and looked out the window to watch dancing shadows on the lawn, made by the wind blowing across treetops, as he stretched his frame to its full five-foot-nine. His dad said he'd grow up to be a bruiser, being that tall already.

He smelled the aroma of his favorite food: Honey-baked ham that his mom was baking for lunch. It was Christmas morning. He threw on his clothes and then ran into the living room. Wendy already sat on the plaid couch playing with her new video game. "Hey, Sissy," he said. "Merry Christmas."

"Morning, Sleepy Head," she said, without looking up, rapidly punching keys with her thumbs, zoned into the digital display of characters dancing on the screen. "And a Merry Christmas to you, too."

He looked and saw the two large boxes beside the spruce Christmas tree. His eyes sparkled brighter than the lights on the tree. He knew what was inside of each box; a weight lifting bench in one, and in the other, a set of weights: a barbell for bench presses, military presses, bent-over rows, squats, and other exercises to build the back, chest, and legs; dumbbells for curls, one-arm rows, butterflies, and many other exercises to build muscles in the arms and other places. Before agreeing to buy him the weights and weight bench for Christmas, his dad had made him learn about body building. He'd read books and surfed the web to learn all he could.

His dad sat in his leather recliner, beer-in-hand. Stan saw him grin as he watched him head toward the boxes. As he yanked off the wrappings, he said, "Thanks Dad."

"Don't hurt yourself with them," his dad said.

His mom walked into the room. Her flowery housecoat and apron was sprinkled with flour and dotted with multicolored smudges of frostings and food coloring. A cigarette dangled from her plump, scarlet red lips. She grasped an imported, green beer bottle in her slender hand. The imports had the best kick, she had once said.

"Merry Christmas, darlings," she said. She sat on the edge of their dad's chair. He placed his muscular arms around her modest waist.

"Merry Christmas, Mom," Stan said. "Thanks for the weights." He knew she had probably talked his dad into buying them for him.

"Well, Ms. Prissy, you can't speak?" her mom said.

Wendy glanced up from her game, cut her eyes in the direction of her mother. "I told you Merry Christmas already, Mamma," she said.

Stan looked at Wendy and rolled his eyes when he saw his dad peek around their mom to stare at her. He knew she couldn't get away with being a smart ass.

"Don't use that tone when you talk to your mother, young lady," her dad said. "It's Christmas. Let's be peaceful today."

"Okay, Dad," Wendy said, and then went back to her game.

Stan made several trips to drag the weights and bench out to the carport, relieved that an episode had been avoided.

That was one of the few days at the house that there hadn't been some kind of fireworks, and it had almost turned out that way, anyway. It would have if their dad hadn't been having a good day. For Christmas, their mom had bought him a Colt, Delta Elite, 10-millimeter pistol. He had wanted one for years but hadn't been able to find one. She had found it, an extra clip, and two boxes of hollow points at a garage sale. It had never been fired. Stan feared their dad would get mad and shoot them with it. He was happy to have his weights to work out with, so he could get started working on becoming a body builder.

For the next four years, he pumped iron five to six days per week, turning his muscles into lean fibers stronger than wire leaders used on deep-sea fishing gear. At sixteen, he had reached six feet tall and weighed 190 pounds, ripped and ready from vigorous exercise routines. His favorite sport was mixed martial arts. Inside the garage he had his own little gym, complete with throw-mats, a speed bag and a heavy bag for practicing kicks and punches, and for using to maintain his coordination. Since receiving his first set of weights at Christmas, he had accumulated additional equipment by doing menial tasks for his neighbors to earn extra money.

Stan and Derrick McCormick were best friends and sparing partners. They worked out and practiced their kicks and punches anytime an opportunity appeared. Even while at school, they'd wrestle and horseplay when they could get away with it; sometimes when they couldn't. In the tenth grade both were suspended from school for horse playing.

Derrick sat in the cafeteria at a long table eating a turkey sandwich and drinking an orange juice. Three other students were huddled on the opposite side of the table, snickering between gulps and bites. Stan crept up behind him, caught him with his mouth full, and moved faster than a mongoose, with the semblance of a snake. He coiled one arm under his neck, locked the hold by grabbing his forearm to apply pressure. Derrick had said he could get loose from the hold without standing, so Stan was testing to see if he had told the truth. "I gotcha now, big boy," Stan said.

Derrick's face turned redder than a ripe cherry as Stan applied more pressure. He reached back to break the lock by attempting to force Stan's hands apart. His elbow struck the table and knocked over everyone's drinks, which attracted the vice principal, Mr. Jenkins, who rushed to the table. "Let go of him, Stan Mason," he said.

Derrick continued resisting and refused to tap out. Stan kept on the pressure. Derrick continued to resist.

"I said to let go of him. I mean it!"

Derrick rapped his knuckles on the table. Stan released the grip, thumped him on the head, and then backed away.

"Both of you. Come with me, now," Mr. Jenkins said.

Stan and Derrick looked at him and then at each other, and then shrugged their shoulders before following him to the Principal's Office, Mr. Stoner.

"Have a seat over there," Mr. Jenkins said, pointing toward four straight-back chairs.

Both sat without comment: Stan to the far right, Derrick to the far left. Mr. Stoner strolled into the room wearing a blue Brooks Brothers suit. His eyes matched the suit. For five or six seconds, he stood by the doorway with his long arms crossed; shifting his focus from one to the other. He knew both from past incidents. He walked within three feet of where they sat, slouched in the chairs.

Stan sat up and tucked the front of his button-down shirt into his jeans. Derrick glanced up at Mr. Stoner but didn't attempt to tighten his attire. He didn't figure he had anything to worry about, since he hadn't gotten out of his seat. Because of the status of his family in the community, he enjoyed the privileges granted to the affluent members of society: scandals forgotten, crimes disposed of, political favors paid in exchange of hefty campaign contributions to the ruling party. His dad was the former City Councilman, and his mother the Mayor of Gwinnett County, Georgia, one of the wealthiest counties in the state.

"Mr. Jenkins says you two don't know where to get your recreation in at," he said. "Does either of you wish to attempt to explain to me why I shouldn't expel you from school for the rest of the year? Both of you know we do not tolerate horseplay in the dining hall."

Derrick sat up. "I didn't do anything wrong," he said.

"I grabbed him," Stan said.

"Mr. Jenkins tells me that you didn't stop when he told you to," he said. "Is that true?"

"I told you I didn't do anything," Derrick said. "Do what you want to do and let me blow this place. I've got more important things to be doing than sitting here listening to you yap, Mr. Stonehead." Derrick evil-eyed him and then said, "You really need to change that name, ... Sir."

16

Mr. Stoner glared at Derrick. "Perhaps that made you feel better," he said. "But, that attitude will cause you numerous problems in life. I don't think your parents approve of it."

"Don't worry about my family," he said.

Stan stood and faced Mr. Stoner. "I told you I started it and that it's my fault, not his."

"Sit down and keep your mouth shut," Mr. Stoner said.

"Fuck you!" Stan said. "Let's go Derrick."

"That's right! Fuck you, Mr. Stone ... head," Derrick said. Then he stood. "We don't have to take any shit from you. You know who my mother is, and you can bet your ass you'll hear from her soon."

"I don't have to take any from you, either," Mr. Stoner said. "Both of you are suspended for two weeks. Feel fortunate that I didn't expel you for the rest of the year." He stepped within a foot of Derrick. "And you, Mr. McCormick, need some lessons that someone will teach you one day, no matter who your mother is."

They continued to rant as they stormed out the door, letting it slam behind them before parading down the hallway, right out the front door of the school. Two weeks later they returned and acted as if nothing had happened. Neither had any more problems at school for the remainder of the year. Later on, Stan moved in with the McCormicks.

◆◆◆◆◆

At almost sixteen Wendy was well-developed for her age. All of the young boys and some of their brothers and fathers stared at her ample breasts and plump rear-end when she strolled through the mall or elsewhere, especially at the swimming pool or lake when she wore her turquoise bikini. Her long blonde hair pulled them toward her; her crystal blue eyes captivated those who dared to get close enough to be lulled in by their radiance. Stan made it clear to the other kids early on not to mess with his sister unless they wanted trouble. Everyone knew he was serious.

For her first date to a rock concert with a dark-haired, buck-toothed, local boy named Terry, she wore an aqua blue halter-top and tight-fitting blue jean short-shorts. She had her hair tied into a ponytail with a blue bandana. Her eyes sparkled brighter than distant stars, as she rushed toward the door, thirty-minutes later than her eleven P.M. curfew. She knew she was in trouble.

Her dad sat in his recliner doing what he had been doing ever since he had came in from work at 3:30 P.M.: drinking beer.

"Come here, you little tramp," he said, when she slid through the sliding-glass door. His words were slurred. "I'm not stupid. I know what you've been out doing with that hoodlum."

A few strands of hair stuck out around her ears. She pushed them back using both thumbs. "You are such a liar," she said, then rolled her eyes, forced out a stream of air.

"I've told you about that smart mouth, young lady," he said. His tone as coarse as sand. Then he grunted, pulled the lever to lower the foot rest, stood. "I'm going to teach you not to talk to me that way."

Stan walked into the living room. Wendy and their dad stood facing each other, arguing.

"Leave me alone!" she said, a second before he slapped her hard enough to knock her sideways.

"I told you about --," he said.

Crack! Stan busted an empty beer bottle across his dad's head. Shards of amber glass glittered on the carpet. In a series of motions that blended into one, his dad stepped backward and turned sharply to elbow him in the face. Stan fell to the ground; blood gushed from his nose.

Wendy screamed. "Stop it, Daddy!"

Their mother ran into the room and saw Stan bleeding, right as his dad kicked him in the side as if trying to kick a field goal at a football game. "Little bastard," he said.

"Darnell, leave that boy alone," their mom said as she ran to the recliner. "What the hell did you do to my boy?"

He raised his foot to stomp Stan and then the distinctive sound of a chambered round echoed throughout the room. He lowered his foot. Temporary silence followed.

She had the Delta Elite aimed at his chest. "If you touch my boy again," she said, struggling to contain the rage, "I'll do what I should have done a long time ago."

"Please don't, Mamma," Wendy said. Tears streamed down her face, leaving streaks of mascara where they ran.

"Edna, you put that gun down," he said. "He busted me in my head with a damn beer bottle. You listen to me woman."

Her hands trembled. She grasped the pistol with both hands to steady it. Her right eye was bruised from their last fight. She tightened her grip on the trigger. The muscles in her face relaxed; her eyes glazed with hate.

"Mamma, please don't," Wendy said. A trickle of blood leaked from the corner of her mouth from the slap.

Stan opened his eyes and wiped the blood from his nose with his shirt-sleeve. "I'm okay, Mamma," he said. Then he sat up and pinched his nose to stop the flow of blood.

The door clanged open. He was back in prison.

CHAPTER 4 – Temporary Absolution

Thirty minutes after the count cleared, Bobby sat on his bed shoveling food into his mouth from a clear plastic bowl when Stan peeked into the cell-door-window. Bobby looked up and motioned with a jerk of his head for him to enter.

"That smells tasty," Stan said. "What is it?"

Between bites, he said, "Rice, refried beans, and a turkey log mixed with Ramen noodles. Want some?"

"I'll pass. Thanks, though. I just stopped by to see what's going on."

"What you going to do about that situation?"

Stan cleared his throat. "Maybe I should listen to you for a change and let it go. Them counting when they did spooked me. Know what I mean?"

"That'd be a good idea. It'll work itself out."

"What's your plans for the day?"

Bobby swallowed the last bite and tossed the spoon and bowl into the sink. "I don't know. What you have in mind?"

"I thought about us getting some laps in. It's a nice day out there now that it stopped snowing."

"All right. That's a bet. Give me a minute to brush my teeth and get dressed for a blizzard, okay?" he said, and then went to the sink.

"See you later," Stan said. He returned to his cell to wait for him to get ready. While there he occupied the time by pacing the floor and primping in the mirror. He had been anxious and narcissistic for most of his life. As a child he never knew what to expect around the house when his parents were drunk or high on drugs. The narcissism probably formed from him pumping iron and flexing his muscles in front of the mirror, as well as from receiving frequent attention from the young girls and cougars, before his arrest on the drug conspiracy case that landed him in prison for ten years.

A staff member's voice boomed over the intercom. "Ten minute move in progress."

"Let's go," Bobby yelled from his cell.

Stan met him on the tier. They rushed for the door to make sure they were out of the cellblock before the move ended. Both wore the prisoner's prized possessions: gray skull caps, sweat pants, sweat shirts; thermal underwear; and camo-green, Vietnam era, army field jackets, complete with inside liners to stop the arctic wind from penetrating. With wind speed often reaching more than 40-miles per hour, and temperatures dropping below zero, jacket liners made a substantial difference in their warmth.

Jacket liners were hard to find because only a few were around. Only the more elite class of prisoners had them: those with money or power. Though neither were wealthy, both made the mark in all categories of the prisoner pecking order, which required either knowing the right people and having their respect, or being feared or trusted enough to climb the ranks. Respect in prison had to be earned: it wasn't given to everyone as a matter of right; without it, integrity and dignity were often taken from the weak by the predators.

Neither Stan or Bobby involved themselves in prison politics unless absolutely necessary, even though each wielded power and had earned the right to vote. They had good reputations and were respected by their peers. Bobby held the most power. Some of it came because of his massive body, but most resulted from his being in prison for the murder of a famous senator's son; the case well-publicized. He had barely escaped the death penalty. Many prisoners hated all politicians for passing Draconian laws, since the early eighties, to get a vote under the guise of reducing recidivism, and for now being too big of a coward to reverse what they knew was a failed experiment. So, for him to have killed one of their family members, it automatically gave him a favorable position in the pecking order. Because he hadn't testified against anyone, the shot-callers knew he would stand for what was right, go down for a good cause without becoming a hated government witness, a rat, despised by most.

Stan's peers accepted and respected him for having fought the guards in a prison riot in Atlanta, at the beginning of his sentence, which resulted in him having served three years in ADX, a control unit at the federal penitentiary in Florence, Colorado. The riot had erupted in the main hallway of the prison, over a protest about guards beating handcuffed prisoners. When the Special Operations Response Team (SORT) stormed the area, wearing full riot gear (protective wear: vests, helmets, shields, pads; wielding weapons; dressed in black outfits with SORT stamped in gold letters), Stan and forty prisoners battled them with fists, feet, and homemade weapons. Many used shanks made of steel, Plexiglas, or plastic, but some used clubs made from plumbing pipes or broken broom handles. SORT members used riot batons, tear gas, pepper spray, stun guns, guns firing rubber bullets or bean bags. After the riot ended, five SORT members were hospitalized for multiple injuries. One had a brain concussion he received after two prisoners wrestled him to the ground; one undid the chin strap and yanked off the helmet, while the other pounded him with a pipe. That's when Stan ran over and kicked another guard in the head, seconds before his involvement ended with 50,000-volts sizzling his circuits, moments before the SORT members had gained control. Two prisoners were dead from guards bashing their heads with riot batons: twelve others hospitalized for various injuries, some of which were incurred when getting dressed out for placement in the hole after the riot had ended. The whole experience had scarred Stan so deeply that it would take years of therapy for him to rise above the hate that saturated his soul. Walking seemed to help him when troubled by thoughts, which is why he wanted to go walk with Bobby that day after the count.

By 9:15 A.M. they were cruising around the asphalt track. Stan's pace neared that of a jogger's as he struggled to keep up with Bobby's racehorse-stride. That's how he liked it: it gave him a good cardiovascular workout. He puffed clouds of condensation as his warm breath mixed with the cold air. He gasped between words as he said, "You're walking me to death, bro."

"You're too soft, pal. Act like a Marine. A motto of theirs is 'When the going gets tough, the tough get going.' So get going and quit whining," he said. Then he chuckled.

Stan pushed harder to stay beside him and then punched him in the biceps. "Hell, I've jogged to stay with you and those long-ass walking sticks you're running on." The air he puffed rolled from his nose and mouth faster than steam from a hot tea kettle. "Get tough," he said, then smirked. "What you mean? I'm already so tough that steal bends when I come near."

"You're a cream puff, pal."

"You kill me with that pal stuff, Pal."

"That's what I mean, Cream Puff. If words can puncture your delicate ego, hammers like these," he said, holding up his fist, "can make you turn to mush in minutes."

"You wouldn't burst a grape if you stepped on it, Sissy."

"Oh, yeah, that's what you say with that alligator mouth and humming bird ass, my friend. You know I'm the meanest S.O.B. this side of the Mississippi," Bobby said. Then he stepped into Stan's path and pushed him off the track into the snow-covered-grass. He stopped and bent over laughing when Stan slipped on the icy edge and fell facedown into the snow.

"You're still a sissy," Stan said, as he got up and brushed the snow and ice off his face and clothes.

Each having gotten in their jeers at the other, they continued to trudge around the track. Only a few other prisoners were on the yard. Even the guard towers looked vacant: They never were. Armed with a variety of weapons to tinker with, the Tower guards were most likely sitting around cleaning their guns, hoping someone would try climbing the forty-foot-wall, so that they could use them for target practice, being the sadistic people some are who work in prisons.

Two miles later Stan said, "Let's take a break."

"All right. Let's go sit up there and kick it for a while before we have to go in for lunch," Bobby said, and pointed toward the bleachers.

"That sounds good to me," Stan said. Then they headed for the top row so they could look beyond the wall at the hills spotted with civilization. After climbing to where they sat, Stan looked at Bobby. "Know what?" he said, without waiting for a response. His forehead was wrinkled. "You mentioning the Marines made me think of dad."

"How you mean?"

"He was proud to have been one and always bragged about how tough they were. His favorite tale was how he had once stopped an Arab from shooting him by pushing on the end of the barrel of a gun. ... A Colt .45, semiautomatic, I believe."

"That's probably what it was because they have a safety mechanism that stops them from firing if you push on the end of the barrel. It pushes the slide back and won't let the trigger work, or something like that."

"Well, I guess that's what he tried with Mom. I didn't go into detail with you about Mom shooting him, but me and Wendy both saw it. It screwed Wendy up real bad."

"How about you? That had to be rough to watch."

Stan took a deep breath before speaking. "Man, I imagine it screwed me up worse than it did her because I blamed myself for Mom having to go to jail for killing the bastard."

He leaned forward and stared into the concrete at a crevice. Bobby watched a couple of prisoners on the far side of the yard horseplay. A Puerto Rican smacked his partner in the back of the head with a snowball and then ran off laughing when his victim dug into the snow for ammo. After a minute or two of silence between them, Stan opened up about the night he wished had never come.

"I was seventeen when it happened," he began. "Wendy came in from a date and dad started calling her names and slapped her when she talked back. I've told you how she is about things like that. She's always had a smart mouth. Anyway, when I saw him smack her, I picked up a beer bottle and hit him in the head. It didn't faze him. He elbowed me in the face and knocked me down. I was out before I hit the carpet," he said. Then he looked over at Bobby and slightly smiled. He was ashamed of what had happened. "I guess he kicked me in the side after that, because I had three broken ribs when taken to the hospital."

"That's really bad, my friend. I feel for you," Bobby said.

"That's nothing. You haven't heard the worst," he said. "Seeing Mom blast him was the bad part. Blood and things splattered all over the living room. Some of it hit me."

"Wow, I can't imagine what that was like for you as a child. It'd be terrible for an adult."

"Have you ever seen what a 170 or 180-grain hollow point does to a man? A lot. When he reached to push back on the barrel, I guess, she stepped back and fired, twice. The first bullet struck him in the jaw and blowed the back, left-side of his head off. The second one hit him above the heart, toward the left shoulder." Stan stopped speaking for a moment and looked at something on the other side of the wall before continuing. "Wendy was screaming and Mom was sobbing, and I don't know what the hell I was doing, besides wondering what to do. The house smelled like copper, gunpowder, and shit. I thought I was going to puke. It just didn't seem real, as if it was some kind of a bad movie playing. All I knew to do was to grab Wendy to hug and hold her until she calmed down. Mom came and joined us." Tears welled in his eyes. "It fucked me up, man. I can still hear and see everything as if it just happened."

"I understand. I'd be fucked up, too. Anyone would."

"It frightened me when the cops came in and then put the cuffs on Mom. I wanted to fight them off and make them leave her alone. But she said for me to look out for Wendy, she'd be okay. ... Me and Wendy had to spend three days in juvenile until Mrs. McCormick could get temporary custody. I told you about her, the mayor of Gwinnett County, Derrick's Mom."

"She must have been a good lady to take y'all in like that," Bobby said.

"Oh, she was. She was really good to us for the whole time we stayed there. Bought us new clothes and carried us wherever we needed to go until her and her husband decided to buy me my first car. The Dodge Durango, I told you about. She's a real sweetheart," he said, and then smiled. "She treated both of us like we were her children. I mean, she knew me real well because of me and Derrick running around together. She didn't know Wendy as good as she did me, but she took to her fast. Wendy liked her, too. They spent a lot of time with each other, having girl talk, you know." Both laughed. "Mrs. McCormick treated us the way I wished Mom had did when we were growing up. Don't get me wrong. I knew Mamma and Daddy both loved us. ... I just think the war messed up Daddy, seeing his buddies get shot and blown up. He didn't talk about it much until he got really drunk, and then he'd sometimes cry when talking about some of the things that had happened. He never really told me and Wendy. I just heard him talking with Mamma about it."

Bobby looked at him and shook his head. "I've ran into a lot of vets in these places over the years. Most of them that I got to know talked about the same type of things happening to them. How screwed up it was to have a partner and have to watch him or her die without being able to help. Maybe that's why so many become dope fiends and alcoholics. You think?"

"Probably so. It's hard to lose someone you're close to, you know? It's tough." Stan said, and then repositioned himself on the concrete slab. "Maybe that had something to do with the way Dad acted toward us. I don't know, really. I just know how hard it was watching my mom kill him. No matter how bad he had treated us, I still loved the crazy bastard."

"How long did you and Wendy stay with the McCormicks?"

"Wendy didn't stay long at all. She married Terry a few months later and moved in with him at his apartment. I stuck around for a little over a year, until Mom won her case on some procedural ground. I think it was actually more because they didn't want to prosecute her in the first place, once they had learned about how he used to beat her."

"That's probably true."

"Anyway, we had lost the house by the time she got out. All she could afford was a small apartment after paying all of the attorney fees, so I moved in with her for a while to help out," Stan said. "I was doing pretty good working as a construction worker on odd jobs with my uncle: painting, slinging a hammer, roofing, laying tile, or whatever he needed."

"I'm sure your Mom really needed for you to be there, to know you didn't hate her for what she had done."

"Oh, she knew how me and Wendy both felt, because we'd go visit her at the jail every visiting day."

"From what I've heard, spending all that time in jail with a bunch of women ain't no joke. A lot of dikes trying to run things can't be fun."

"The McCormicks offered to help her in any way they could, but she wouldn't accept anything because of all they had done for me and Wendy. She did let Mrs. McCormick get her a good job with the county."

"That's good."

"Yeah, it was. She had stopped drinking after going to a meeting in jail for alcoholics. Going to work every day without drinking away her money, helped her get the things she needed to take care of herself better than I had ever seen. She even started going to the gym and working out. Anyway, she met a lot of good people through her work with social services, and at the gym. That's where she met my step-dad two years later, at the gym."

A few minutes later they had to go back inside for the count. When walking down the long corridor, Stan saw Jake on the opposite end, clearing the corner going toward the cellblock. The sight of him re-ignited the rage behind the resentment. "There goes the snake," Stan said.

Bobby put his big arm over Stan's shoulder. "What happened to letting it go?"

"Maybe it was just temporary absolution," he said, "because I am right back to hating the bastard."

A minute later they walked into B-Lower behind Jake, where the three of them lived.

PART II

Mr. D

CHAPTER 5 – Wendy

"Yes, darling, I will be there for the holiday weekend in July," she said. "I plan on catching a flight in Atlanta on Thursday evening, and then renting a car at the airport in Kansas City. The room at the hotel is already reserved."

"All right. Make sure you're here early, okay," Terry said. "Gotta go. I'm about out of phone minutes."

"Do you need me to send you some money?"

"Yeah baby, I do. Send me what you can. All right. I'll call again, soon. Love ya, babe."

"Love you, too," she said.

She hung up the phone and popped another grape into her mouth before going to the bedroom to get ready for bed. It had been a long day of staring at the computer screen and manipulating data to make the system work better for its many users. Her favorite time of the evening was after stripping off her office attire and climbing into the Jacuzzi to relax. She'd lay in the warm water and caress away the stress of the day, wishing Terry was there with her. Life seemed unfair at times. Being married to a man in prison was tough. At least Stan was at the same prison and helped look out for him. When she visited the next time, she'd get to see both while there. Terry wanted her to call him out alone on the first day, said he needed to talk about something important; probably what he had mentioned before, helping him make some money. Though he hadn't said so, she figured it was something to do with drugs. She hung her clothes on the hooks and climbed into the warm water, closed her eyes, and tried to forget the day.

The next morning, sunlight streamed through the spaces between the slats of the venetian blinds. Moments after doing her daily rituals that included meditation and exercise, she stopped by the kitchen and picked up her Swiss Mocha made by the automated coffee pot program. In the bathroom, standing in her aqua-blue negligee, she put on her face in front of her full-length mirror, slowing only to sip mocha.

Twenty minutes later she admired her work. A little more eyeliner, she thought, and she'd be ready to go. Perfect! I'm still a doll. After getting dressed, she stopped by the mirror on her vanity. I've got to do something about this, she said, when she glimpsed at the freckles scattered between her breasts. She adjusted her blouse to cover them, positioned her skirt on her full-hips; noticed a flaw on her lips, added another dab of pink lipstick. One more thing, the fish. She rushed to the aquarium in the living room and called each fish by its name as she sprinkled food into the tank. Then she grabbed her purse and hurried out the door to her old Mazda RX-7. The rotary engine growled when she revved it a few times. Then she pushed in her favorite CD by Pink before pushing the button and opening the garage. As soon as she reached the roadway, she floored it.

Nicole would be cursing if she was late for their brunch-date at the restaurant in the mall, five miles from her house. The tires barked as she hit first and then second gear. Once she had went through the other gears, the engine purred as she zoomed by the oaks, magnolias, and dogwood trees that lined the streets. She kept an eye on her Fuzz Buster because with the stereo blaring, she might not hear it go off as she sang *"Fuckin Perfect"* with Pink.

Nicole had divorced her abusive husband two years before, and consistently urged her to do the same with Terry. "He's a loser, babe. Drop him like a rock," she'd say. Wendy had thought about it often. He hadn't mistreated her because he knew what Stan would do to him if he did. Stan warned him before they were married that he would die an agonizing death if he hurt her, so she never worried about that aspect of their relationship. He just seemed more concerned with her helping support his dope habit than anything else. Even before he went to prison, he was bad about getting money from her, which made her feel as if he was taking advantage of her. She didn't want to acknowledge that her marriage had failed, just as her parent's had several years before her mom shot her dad. It was more than what she wanted to admit.

She parked beside Nicole's Ford Focus. Nicole smiled and got out to meet her when she opened the door. "What's up, girlfriend?" Wendy said.

Nicole grinned. "You know, same ole, same ole. Still looking for my knight in shining armor," she said. "He's still managing to elude me."

"Keep looking, Love. He can't hide forever. You'll catch him one day and sink those claws into him so he'll never get away." Both laughed and then hugged before going inside to find a table.

When the automated sliding glass doors popped open, Wendy inhaled deeply and then said, "Nothing makes me hungrier than the sweet smell of pancakes and bacon on a grill."

"Let's sit there," Nicole said, pointing at a corner booth as the host approached them with menus in his hand. She surveyed his body. "We got this, babe," she said. Both smiled at him and sashayed to the booth. Nicole glanced over her shoulder for a second look and smiled when she caught him watching. Once out of ear reach, she said, "I'd teach that one some lessons on loving a cougar, faster than he could get my panties off."

"You are so terrible," Wendy said, blushing.

"Not terrible. In heat," she whispered, and then grinned. "I need action, doll. I haven't been laid in three whole days."

Wendy liked that Nicole was straight-forward with her, even when her comments embarrassed her. She smiled and then teased, "You are such a slut, darling, but at least you put it out in the open."

"How else can I get what I want? Have any referrals, honey?" she said, as she touched Wendy's right arm.

Wendy winked at her. "One day, maybe I'll find you one you'll keep, instead of using him for your wicked pleasures and then fleeing. Your undeniable modus operandi, right?"

Nicole rolled her eyes and laughed. "What better way is there to do it?" she said. Then they grabbed a seat at the booth. Nicole adjusted her blouse to reveal more cleavage before the waiter arrived, making sure he'd have a better view of her 38 double-D's. "I like that one there," she said, nodding toward a tall, young, muscular man with deep-set eyes, high cheekbones, and raven hair.

"He's a cute one," Wendy said. "Maybe he has the total package to quench your thirst and satiate that lustful desire." She fluffed her hair in mock fashion and beamed when Nicole giggled and smiled.

The waiter Nicole had commented on, turned and started walking toward their table. Nicole crossed her legs: Her red skirt moved slightly up. "I'm such a lucky girl," she said. "Here comes my fantasy."

"He's ten years younger than you."

"Good. Maybe he can keep up with me when I get those clothes off."

Wendy leaned closer and whispered, "He might be more than you can handle," and then giggled.

He approached the table with his order pad in hand, and then stood closer to the side where Nicole sat. "Good morning," he said. "What may I get you two lovely ladies?"

Nicole scooted forward and watched his eyes follow the hem of her skirt before shifting to her breast. When he smiled she noticed straight, white, evenly spaced teeth; and then no wedding ring on his finger. Wendy said, "I'll have a cup of Swiss Mocha, blueberry pancakes, bacon, and hash browns, smothered and covered."

Nicole peered into his caramel brown eyes and then smiled. "I'll have the same if you come with it."

He chuckled and then said, "Aren't you direct."

"A closed mouth doesn't get fed, precious," she said.

He winked, and then said, "I guess you're right on that. We'll talk later. Right now, I'll get your orders."

He rushed from the table but then looked back and smiled broadly when he made eye contact with Nicole. He shook his head and almost bumped into another waiter. He glanced one more time and disappeared behind a swinging door.

Wendy's cheeks turned a rose-colored pink. "Nicole, what am I going to do with you? There's not an ounce of shame in your game, is there?" she said, as she dabbed dots of perspiration on her forehead with a napkin.

Nicole squeezed her thighs against each other, creating a tingling sensation. "You think he wants me?"

"The way his eyes disrobed you, and with that big smile he gave when he looked back, you may get lucky, girl. He's real interested. I just don't know how you can expose yourself that way. It terrorizes me for a man to look at me the way he stood scrutinizing your two cantaloupes."

"That's why I bought them. I love the reaction they get from young studs. With me approaching forty, I need every edge I can get. Hell, if you got laid again you might understand. It's been so long for you that it might not even open anymore." She tapped Wendy's foot with hers and snickered.

Wendy ignored her snide comments because she knew Nicole wanted to talk about her divorcing Terry. "You don't worry about getting something you're not looking for, like herpes, or about ending up with some sicko in the sack?"

"Can't say I am, dear. You know I use protection and can take care of myself. I had a great self-defense instructor."

The waiter arrived with their Swiss Mocha. Wendy read his name tag. "Thank you, Moses," she said, when he placed a napkin on the table and sat down her cup.

"You're welcome," he said, leaving the last vowel open. When she didn't say her name, he turned to Nicole and did the same with napkin and cup. "What may I call you, dear?"

"Nicole. Thank you," she said, accepting her beverage. "I'm Nicole and that's Wendy."

"You are both very lovely ladies. I am honored to meet you," he said, bending slightly forward at the waist. "I'll return with your order in a moment." Then he turned and went to wait on two couples, whom the host seated closer to the front of the restaurant.

Nicole opened her eyes wide. "I think he liked you."

"I'm not interested. You know I'm married and don't cheat on him."

"If he were out here, and you were in there, do you really believe that he wouldn't be screwing every woman and girl he could find?"

"He might," she said, twisting a napkin in her hand. "Probably would, but that doesn't make it right for me to do it, does it?"

"I don't think anyone would hold it against you if you did," Nicole said. Then she sipped her mocha.

"My dad mistreated my mother the whole time he was alive, and probably cheated on her, too," she said. "But Mamma never cheated on him and I don't think I should cheat on Terry, either, even if he is in prison and may deserve it."

"I'm sorry, doll, but I still say you should drop him. Don't waste another day on the loser. Give yourself a break. Why do you stick with him, anyway?" she said, and continued speaking without slowing down. "You've already waited five years, and from what I've seen, all he does is ask you to send him money, or to do something for him. What about Wendy?"

Moses returned with their orders, terminating their conversation about Terry. After a brief casual conversation, he slid Nicole a slip of paper with his number on it. She smiled. "I'll call you tonight, handsome," she said. He smiled at both and walked away, leaving the bill on the table, which Wendy paid after eating. Nicole left a $20.00 tip. She got laid that night. Wendy went home to sleep alone and plan for her visit with Terry and Stan.

CHAPTER 6 – Let It Go

Months later, on a cool spring morning, Stan and Bobby returned from the yard and took their showers before being counted at 10 A.M. Shortly thereafter, they went to eat Spanish omelets, oatmeal, biscuits and gravy for brunch. That afternoon, Stan sat near the center of the TV room watching VH1. The TV room was on the walkway at the rear of the cellblock that joined the tiers. Terry, Jake, and three of Jake's friends were huddled in the back corner. Two Jamaicans, who were acquaintances of Stan, sat closest to the only door, talking. Stan lowered the volume on his Walkman to hear Jake and Terry's conversation. A few minutes later his suspicion was confirmed: Terry still planned to involve Wendy.

"She's coming over the holiday weekend in July and I'll talk her into bringing in the package," Terry said.

Stan stood and turned to face all five in the corner. "Keep my sister's name out of your mouth," he said.

"Keep out of my business, boy," Jake said. Him and his three friends stood. Terry stayed seated.

"Don't try fucking with this boy!" Stan said.

Terry stood. "I won't let anything happen to her, dude," he said, his voice a high-pitched tone, almost a shrill.

Rastaman stepped out the door and cleared the corner of the tier to get Big Bobby. At the same moment, Bobby walked out of his cell to go get some hot water. Rastaman saw him and yelled in his Jamaican accent. "Yo, mon, Stan need you." Bobby slung the cup in his cell.

One of Jake's partners positioned himself near the door by the other Jamaican, who sat looking toward the television with a know-nothing stare on his face.

"You're damn right you're not because you're not going to pull her into your shit," Stan said. "Find another way to feed your habit."

Jake's other partners tried to position themselves behind Stan, who turned to put the wall behind him. Jake moved closer to him and said, "What's up? You want to get this out of the way, right now?"

"Smash that punk!" the one by the door said.

Terry edged closer to the door. "Y'all cut this bullshit out, dudes," he said. "We'll all go to the hole."

Jake moved within arm's reach. Stan shoved him in the chest with both palms. "Get off me, punk," he said. Jake stumbled backward.

He regained his balance and rushed back to get in Stan's face. "Want some of this," he said, and pushed him back.

"Don't take that from that cunt," another yelled. "Hit him!"

The one by the door pulled a shank from his waistband. "Let's stick this bitch," he said, his back a foot from the door.

Everything changed fast: Big Bobby barged into the room. The door smacked the doorman holding the shank, knocked him into Terry, who shot to the wall near Bobby.

"Hey," the doorman shouted, as he turned to see who had hit him with the door. His face paled when he saw Bobby. He hurried beside Jake, faced Bobby.

Jake had moved to the corner when Bobby rushed into the room. "What's up?" Bobby said, his voice coarse.

The two who had surrounded Stan moved with Jake. Terry stood against the wall with his arms crossed. Bobby moved within striking distance of the doorman.

"Let it go, man," he said. Rastaman had followed him into the room. The other Jamaican stood and positioned himself beside his partner and Bobby.

Stan eyed the two who tried getting behind him, and then he moved near Bobby and the Jamaicans. He looked at the one with the shank. "Put that up before I stick it up your ass," he said.

"You got the easy part done," the doorman said.

"Cut the bullshit," Terry said.

Still winded from rushing down the tier, Bobby said, "All of you need to put this on ice. Nothing good's going to come from us going to war over whatever the hell y'all got going on in here."

Jake took a step closer to them. "Tell your boy to keep out of my business, big guy."

Bobby started to speak. Stan pointed at Terry. "I've done told that idiot I didn't want him involving my sister in your business, buddy," he said. "If you can't respect that, we've got big problems."

"You've got big problems with all that mouth," the doorman said. Seconds earlier, he had slipped the blade of the shank in the front pocket of his pants and covered its handle with his hand.

"Look man, my problem's not with you but we can make it that way if you don't back off," Stan said. He moved closer to him. "I don't give a damn about you having a shank."

Bobby stepped between Stan, Jake, and the doorman. The Jamaicans stayed in the background, propped against the wall by the door where Terry stood. The doorman jerked out the shank. Before Bobby could stop him, Stan maneuvered around him and grabbed the doorman's wrist holding the shank. In a continuous motion, he twisted it behind the man's back and yanked it to the base of the neck, as he forced him against the rear wall. "What you want to do now, bitch?" Stan growled, keeping the pressure on the back of his prey.

Jake advanced toward Stan. Bobby grabbed him by the shoulders and slung him against the wall, and then turned his head to glance at the other two, making sure they weren't getting involved. "Stay out of it!" he said.

The Jamaicans, who were much larger than either of the two they faced, had moved between them and Bobby. Both Jamaicans had their arms spread, angled toward the floor, palms opened, inviting war or peace. "We don't want no trouble," one of the other two said.

After he had failed to free himself from Stan's hold, the doorman dropped the shank. It clanged as it struck the floor. "All right, man. You got it." he said, his voice strained from stress.

Jake stayed still against the wall, fear written on his forehead: Bobby's massive chest six inches from his nose.

Stan used his foot to slide the shank to the far side of the room. Then he released his hold and stepped away from the doorman. "Let's all let this shit go and get the fuck out of here before the hacks come and slam us in the hole," he said.

Everyone exited the television room; their eyes darting one from another, sweat dotting their foreheads. Stan waited until last to leave, motioning for the doorman to get his shank and go. He did so silently, his head held low.

Five minutes after leaving the TV room, Stan had told Bobby all that had went down before he walked into the drama. They sat in Stan's cell with their arms crossed, sodas sitting on the floor by each of their legs. Neither one uncrossed their arms except to take a sip from their sodas.

"What you think about it?" Stan said. "You think they're going to let it go or what?"

Bobby cleared his throat and then repositioned himself on the toilet bowl where he sat. "I'd like to think that they'll let it go and leave us alone, but you know how things go in these places. They may claim a truce only to gain an edge for an attack. I'm going to keep an eye on 'em, for sure."

"You know I'll keep an eye on them. And if Terry and Jake don't leave Wendy out of their plans, they'd better keep an eye on me," Stan said, and then got up from the edge of his bed. "I'm telling you, man, if they don't, it's going to be bad. Wendy may become a widow before it's over with if they don't."

"Well, ... we'll just have to play the cards dealt and play the game well. Let it go if you can," Bobby said. Then he rose and patted Stan on the back. "Gotta go, Pal. Keep your eyes open. Yell if you need me, okay?"

"Okay, man. I'm sorry I got you into this bullshit."

"Don't sweat it. It'll all work itself out however the hell it's supposed to turn out." Then he ducked to leave the cell. He stopped on the tier.

"See you later," he said and threw up his hand before walking back to his cell.

CHAPTER 7 – Big Bobby

He knew not to lie down and go to sleep with the doors open, after having had an altercation with other prisoners, so he sat on his bed to read a magazine until count time. Sometimes it seemed as if all they did in prison was to stand and get counted. The federal prison system must be ran by a bunch of paranoid people, he thought, as he opened the magazine and began flipping through its pages to free his mind of what had happened. He didn't like renting mind-space to a possible attack, but he knew it was a necessary survival skill in the insane world of incarceration, for someone to remain mindful of a retaliatory attack after having had a conflict. The wise ones realized that the mundane existence of a person in prison often lulled them to sleep: sometimes with fatal consequences. He didn't want to go out that way. Even though he had life without parole, he didn't want his life to end at the hands of some psychopath with a shank. Like many of his peers, he hoped for a change in the laws that would allow him to walk out the door one day as a free man. That wasn't something he spoke about often, nor did he routinely entertain the thought of it, since he didn't want to spend his days dreaming of something that most likely would never happen. Without hopes and dreams, though, there wasn't much left for a man sentenced to die in prison. Freedom was something he hoped for without much faith in having it again.

Under normal circumstances, he tried to stay in the moment, not to dwell on the past, or to dream about the future. It was better that way. Today the past haunted him. The magazine had an article about Senator Leroy Johnson, whose son he was in prison for murdering, Roger Johnson. He stopped reading and did what he had done countless times, tried remembering what had happened that night. All he recalled was getting into the Mercedes with him to go cruising and partying. Hell, the man was his friend. They had graduated together at the same university; Roger in Political Science, Bobby in Sociology. The night Roger was murdered, he thought they'd stopped at a titty bar for a few drinks and lap dances, but that's where the neurons and synapses malfunctioned in the memory retrieval process. Roger and he had been having a blast playing with the girls. Most of the dancers knew who Roger's dad was, and that Roger had lots of cash that he loved spending, so they flocked to their table with hopes of romance and plenty of laughs.

The next day he had awakened at the apartment of a girl in Charlotte, NC, with no idea of how he'd gotten there, who she was, or what they had done. He barely remembered her. What he recalled was that she was beautiful, and the embarrassment he had felt for not knowing her name and then having to ask.

"Sheila," she had said, "you don't remember anything at all?" He had felt like a worm.

He regretted not remembering what she had said they had done that night: lots of drinking and lots of kinky sex, but there wasn't much to do about it besides to try it again, which they had planned on doing. The FBI ruined those plans. She had driven him to his apartment the next day. When he stepped out of her Escalade, he said, "Tomorrow evening we'll go out and party till our clothes come off. I promise." The FBI arrested him before they could meet and he never saw her again.

He was sitting there thinking of her when Stan came to the door and startled him by speaking.

"Hey, man, what's up? You're awful jumpy."

"Not much," he said. "Sitting here reminiscing about Sheila. You know, that girl I was with the night before the feds busted into my life and took me hostage." He held up the magazine. "There's an article in this about Senator Johnson and it got me started thinking, which you know is dangerous." He smiled as he handed it to Stan.

"What's it about?" he said, before he started flicking through the pages and looking at pictures.

"I've read most of it but not everything. From what I've seen, it's all about his re-election campaign, some new tough-on-crime bills he's pushing to introduce, and the typical political bullshit."

"What's up with you and Sheila? You ever figure out how to find her?"

"If I could remember her last name, then I could try having someone to find her on the Internet." He paused for a moment and then said, "I'd sure like to see her again. Maybe she'd be able to tell me more about what had happened that night. I was still hung-over when she carried me home. ... I really don't remember much of what she told me I had done, other than that I had made it good to her when we fucked." Then he smiled. "Hell, I thought it was funny that I couldn't remember anything. Now I don't. Those blackouts aren't anything to joke about. That's why I quit drinking. I can't afford not to know what I'm doing inside these places. Know what I mean, bro?"

"Yeah, I do. I've been there, too. Woke up in some of the damndest places and not have a clue about how I had gotten there or what I'd did. One time, I lost three days by eating a handful of Valiums and drinking Hurricanes. Scared the hell out of me. I could have done the same thing as you and not even known it. Hell, I may have. I don't know."

Bobby nodded his head. "What's up with Wendy? Have you talked to her lately?"

"Not in the last few days. I'm afraid to say too much over the telephone because I don't want S.I.S. involved in our business. It's a miracle no one told about what happened in the TV room."

"They still might. You know how Inmate.com works in these places. Before it's over with, the word on the compound will be that someone got murdered or stabbed in there. Hopefully, it won't make it to the cops, but you know how guys like to talk. Can't keep a secret."

"Maybe we'll get lucky," Stan said. He laid the magazine on the locker. "She's supposed to be coming to visit before long. I'll talk to her then. ... Man, if he tries to get her to do that bullshit, I will beat his brains out."

"What you think we need to do about Jake?"

"You know what I think. I still want to put his lights out. I don't like anything about him, period."

"Well, I know that, but do you think I need to go talk to him and let him know it's squashed, as far as I'm concerned?"

"Really, all of us need to get together and work things out," Stan said, "rather than walk around sweating each other. I don't like being stressed out, having to worry about some idiot sneaking up and stabbing me in the kidney."

"This type of drama is what I hate most about prison. Sometimes our only choice is which evil is best. That really sucks," Bobby said. He stood and picked up the magazine. "Knowing the way things go for me, I'd pick up another case and then win this one and have to stay in prison because of the new one."

"Let's not go there. I damn sure don't need another one, and if you get one, then you know I'll have one too," he said. He looked at Bobby and grinned. "Hell, if you get one, it'll be because of me, and I damn sure don't want that to happen. You're a good man and don't need to spend the rest of your life in these places."

Bobby laid down the magazine. Then he shook hands with Stan, before he gently patted him on his back, as was his usual way of showing affection in a place devoid of normal emotional responses. "I appreciate it. Too bad the powers-that-be don't agree."

"Maybe they will one day," Stan said. Then he walked back to his cell.

CHAPTER 8 – Stan

◆◆◆◆◆

Derrick knocked on Stan's bedroom door. "Get up out of that bed," he said from the hallway. "Let's go cruising and see what we can bring home with us tonight."

Stan rolled over. "What time is it?"

Derrick opened the door but didn't enter. "Eight o'clock. There should be plenty of girls out running around the mall by now. It's Friday night, man."

"I know what day it is. I'm just tired. We tore down patios and balconies today at the apartment complex we're remodeling in Jonesboro, and I'm wore out."

"Come on, man. Mom and Dad are out of town for the weekend and we can bring 'em back here if we hook any, and you know we will," he said and then smiled. "Hell, they can't resist studs like us."

Stan got out of the bed. "All right. Give me a few and I'll be ready to roll. You're buying tonight."

"It's a deal," Derrick said, and then closed the door.

After washing his face and then putting on his favorite jeans and pullover shirt, Stan met Derrick in their usual place for socializing with each other in the house, the dining room. Derrick sat rolling a joint at the smoked-glass dining room table. "Fire it up," Stan said.

"This is that same kind of skunk bud Henry had last night," he said. "Red and blue-haired-sens."

Stan picked up a bud and sniffed it. "I love the pine needle scent."

"Me, too," Derrick said. "We'll burn these later," he said, sticking two joints in his shirt pocket. Then he handed Stan a bong. "Here, load this."

An hour later they were cruising the Mall in Derrick's red Dodge Viper. A wide array of reds, blues, greens, yellows, and white lights emblazoned cars and buildings. Hundreds of multicolored cars of numerous makes and models lingered along the main strip of the Mall, dotting the parking lot and roadways surrounding the shopping center and neighboring businesses. Occupants in the cars waved at friends or gave foes the finger, as they met oncoming traffic. A vast assortment of music blared from stereos. Many drivers honked their horns. Derrick and Stan cruised along and jammed on Three Doors Down while they scanned the area for girls of interest. The sleekness of the Viper and the rumble of its powerful engine always succeeded at attracting attention.

"Check 'em out," Derrick said, with his left arm hanging out the window. He pointed at a redhead and a brunette in a dark-blue, BMW Z-4 roadster, in the opposite lane, easing along the lines of traffic on the main strip, coming toward them.

"Aren't they the ones from the movie last week?" Stan said. "They're some nice ones, for real."

The week before, Spider-Man 2 had opened at the theater, and they had briefly met each other before exiting the building.

"Yeah, that's them. I think their names were Jasmine and Veronica," Derrick said. "The redhead's Jasmine, right?"

"That's right, man. She's mine," Stan said. He smiled and playfully punched Derrick's shoulder.

When the nose of their cars were within a few yards of each other, Derrick tapped the horn. Jasmine glanced their way and waved, and then Veronica did the same. Everyone was smiling when the cars were side-by-side.

"Hey, what's up with y'all beautiful maidens tonight?" Derrick said.

"Not much. Just out having fun," Jasmine said.

"Meet us at the Burger King in five minutes if you want to really have some fun," he said.

Veronica rose up in her seat as the cars passed. "Okay, we'll be there," she said. Then she smiled and waved.

Jasmine threw up her hand and waved as she revved the engine, and then she made the tires bark. Both of them turned around, giggling. Derrick reciprocated by stopping the flow of traffic, and then power-breaking as he burned the tires for a couple of seconds. Clouds of smoke covered the cars. He turned off the main strip and zipped through the parking lot en route to the Burger King on the other side of the Mall, two miles away.

Working their way through the traffic, Derrick looked over at Stan and smiled. "I told you," he said. "We're on, I'll bet you."

Stan ran his hand through his hair. "I hope you're right. I really like what I see. She has to be one of the loveliest girls I've ever seen. Know what I mean?"

"Don't tell me you're in love already."

"Okay, how about in lust?"

"I'll go for that," he said, and then both laughed. Jasmine and Veronica sat in the Z4 waiting, backed into a slot on the back row of the parking lot, when they arrived. Derrick pulled in beside them. Jasmine smiled at Stan before he could speak. "What y'all got planned tonight?" he said.

"Not a lot," Jasmine said. "Just out to have a little fun on the town, you know."

"Want to burn one of these big bombers?" Derrick said. He held up a joint. "It's red and blue-haired-sens."

"Hell, yeah," both girls said at the same time, and then looked at each other and giggled. "Where you want to do it?" Veronica asked.

"Follow us. My parents are out of town and we have the house for the weekend," Derrick said.

When they had met at the theater, he had told them who his parents were, as was his habit. It seemed to make girls feel safer with them.

Fifteen minutes later they pulled in the long-winding driveway leading to his parent's Victorian style mansion. Jasmine climbed out wearing an apricot V-neck tunic, light denim jeans, and tennis shoes. Veronica had on denim stretch jeans, tennis shoes, and an Ivory, embroidered tee-shirt with a sweetheart neck that contrasted perfectly with her light brown flesh.

"Hi Sugar," Veronica said, as she gently tugged the bottom of her shirt. Her dark brown nipples showed through the ivory-colored fabric, which heightened her sexuality.

"What's up sugar britches," Derrick said, his eyes locked on her breasts. She ran her tongue across her luscious lips and then smiled.

"Let's go to the pool," Stan said.

Derrick and Veronica were transfixed on each other and didn't respond.

"Sounds like a wonderful idea to me," Jasmine said. She grabbed Stan's hand. He glanced back at the other two and saw they were occupied, so he led her on a tour through the house, allowing her to stop and admire all of the beautiful fixtures and elegant settings.

"Want something to drink?" he asked.

"What do you have?"

"We have all sorts of sodas, mango, orange or grapefruit juice, and some liquor: Jack Daniels, Jim Beam, Crown Royal, and Seagrams Seven. We've got it hidden. We had to pay someone to buy it. The McCormicks don't drink much alcohol, so me and Derrick pay an older man to get it for us. We give him a little weed or a few pills, and he'll get what we want."

"Do you mind making me a bourbon and Coke?"

"Don't mind at all, sweetheart," he said, a smile creased his lips. He pulled her to him and then kissed her for the first time. A fireworks show exploded inside his head when their lips met. He knew she'd be his wife.

They stopped by the refrigerator for the Coke. He pulled out the Jack Daniels from under the sink and got four glasses from the cabinet. "Let's go to the patio," he said. "If you will carry the glasses, I'll carry the rest."

Derrick put his arm around Veronica's slender waist and pulled her close to softly kiss her below the ear. Chills coursed throughout her body. She shivered and then turned to face him for a hug and a kiss. He noticed goose bumps on her delicate flesh; smiled and pulled her closer for the kiss. Afterward, she said, "You are a wonderful kisser. We'll definitely have us some fun tonight, if you use those lips and that tongue the same way all the time." She batted her eyelashes and simultaneously used her right hand to fan her face. Her honey-brown eyes twinkled as she flashed her bright white teeth and then pursed her lips for another kiss.

"Damn right, we will, baby doll." With his hands on her firm hips, he pulled her until their pelvis bones met. They kissed again, much longer this time. He couldn't believe how lucky he had gotten by Stan choosing Jasmine. Both were real lookers and very intelligent, but what he loved most about Veronica was her lively spirit and radiant personality, as well as her velvety, creamy-chocolate skin.

A few minutes later they met Stan and Jasmine on the patio. Stan had the bottle of Jack Daniels and the two-liter bottle of Coke sitting on the table. All four drank liquor, smoked the joints Derrick had rolled, and then swam in the sparkling water before going to the bedrooms. Jasmine got pregnant that night: They married before the baby was born.

Before they had married, they met wherever they could. Since Derrick and Veronica were their best friends, they were usually with them or close-by. For the first week they mainly met at the Mall or at one of the local swimming holes. With Mr. & Mrs. McCormick in town, they couldn't party at their house, so they'd go to the river or to a house or an apartment of one of their friends. And then Veronica persuaded her parents into allowing them to use their cabin on Lake Sidney Lanier, north of Atlanta. Her parents were laid-back and not real controlling. Before her dad agreed, he met with all four to let them know the conditions. "If y'all go there, I expect you to act responsibly by not drinking, and certainly not while driving or swimming. I don't want anyone's death on my conscience, or to have to pay for your funerals," he said. "I also expect you to keep it clean, treat it like it's yours," and then he stopped and laughed. "On second thought, maybe a little better than that." He remembered Veronica's messy bedroom when she was younger.

All four loved the lake. The cabin sat in a cove, where they would stay for the weekends and have cookouts, swim, and sometimes fish, water ski, or wind surf. Sometimes, though, they'd venture out to the less frequented areas that the Army Corps of Engineers had cut into various places around the 700 plus-miles of shoreline.

Because neither Derrick's Viper or Jasmine's Z4 was made for rough terrain, everyone had climbed into Veronica's Honda CR-V and went to a spot near the Buford Dam. The July sun beamed brightly, casting its scorching rays down upon their young bodies, as all four laid on beach towels and blankets and soaked up the sun. For the sake of privacy, Stan and Jasmine were on one side of the hollow, Derrick and Veronica on the other. A partially submerged oak tree protruded from the water, about thirty yards from where Derrick and Veronica stayed.

During one of the public work projects created by President Roosevelt to revive the economy, when making Lake Lanier, numerous laborers cut down trees in the valley where the Chattahoochee River rushed south toward Atlanta. The Buford Dam tamed its flow and made the lake. Hundreds of trees lay beneath the surface of the water. Snakes like trees. Cottonmouth Moccasins like trees and water.

Derrick rolled over and slapped Veronica on her butt. "Come on, baby. Let's go swimming," he said. Then he pointed toward the oak. "I want to go out there to that log and smoke this joint." He sat up and started wrapping it and a blue BIC lighter in a plastic sandwich bag.

"Why you wanna go out there," she said. "What's wrong with smoking it here?"

"No particular reason. Just want to do something unusual, baby doll."

"Let's do it, then," she said, as she pushed herself up. She stood and brushed off some pine needles stuck to the suntan oil on her shapely legs, and then moved in for a long kiss; wrapped her arms around his waist. "The things I'll do for love amazes me, sometimes."

He cupped the cheeks of her butt with both hands and pulled her close as their tongues did the tango. By the time they stopped he was googly-eyed. "Damn it, girl," he said. "You're spoiling me with kisses like that. Keep that up and you'll never get rid of me."

"Who said I want to get rid of you? I'm loving it as much as you," she said. Then she ran her hands up his back and through his hair before she kissed the tip of his nose. "You're not bad for a white boy."

Both laughed and began running toward the water. He let her get ahead so he could watch the seductive sway of her hips in the white thong bikini. He loved the contrast between the white fabric and her flesh. "Let's race," he said.

A slight cliff was at the water's edge where they dove in and swam for the log. Veronica won the race. She straddled the log and held out her hand to pull him into her grasp for more hugs and kisses. After his hands had dried, he pulled out the bag and fired the joint. "Give me a shotgun," she said. When he did, she coughed and lost the toke. The whites of her eyes reddened. "Oh, honey, that was a good one," she said. Then she giggled.

"Want another one?"

"You know I do."

The pain struck his right leg as he started blowing. He jerked the joint from his mouth and grimaced in pain.

"What's wrong?" she said.

"I think something bit me," he said as he reached down to feel where it hurt. "My god, it's a snake!" The water moccasin still had its fangs buried in his skin, below the calf. He grabbed it behind its head. "Get back," he said and pushed her away before he pulled the three-foot-long serpent from the water. "It's a damn cottonmouth."

She peddled in the water away from the log, her eyes wide open. "Are you okay?"

"Stay over there until I get rid of it and then swim for the shore," he said. He threw the snake into deeper water. She swam toward him. He waited for her and then they swam together toward the bank.

"Stan, Jasmine," she screamed between breaths.

"I'm okay," he said. "I'll be all right."

When they reached the bank he yelled for Stan.

Stan and Jasmine simultaneously raised their heads. "Did you hear that?" Stan said.

"It sounded like Derrick," she said, and then they heard him again.

"Yeah, man. What's going on over there?" Stan shouted.

"Come on, we've got to go," Derrick yelled. "I got bit by a water moccasin."

Stan and Jasmine jumped up, grabbed their belongings, and jogged to where Derrick laid on a blanket and beach towel. Veronica had put it down for him before going for her Blackberry. She stood a few feet away speaking on the phone with her dad when they ran up to Derrick.

Still panting from running, Stan said, "You okay, man?"

"Kind of weak and nauseated," he said, "but I think I'll be all right if you get me to the hospital."

"We'll get you there, buddy," Stan said.

Veronica walked over to them. "Okay. I'll ask him to do it. I'll call you back," she said, and then hung-up. "Dad said to get the First Aid kit from the spare tire compartment. That there's a snake bite kit inside of it. Please run and get it for me, if you will. I've got to call 9-1-1."

"All right, I'll be right back," Stan said, then hurried to the CR-V.

"Hi, I'm Veronica Calhoun. My boyfriend was bit by a cottonmouth water moccasin, a few minutes ago. We're about three or four miles above the Buford Dam on Lake Lanier and need to get him to a hospital. Can you have an ambulance to meet us somewhere? ... Okay. ... Yes, we have a snake bite kit. ... Yes, I know not to cut the wounds. My dad is a doctor and has already told me what to do and what not to do, but I appreciate you letting me know. ... Okay. ... All right. I'll meet him on Highway 20. We'll be in a silver Honda CR-V. Thank you," she said.

After she hung-up, she said, "We need to get him in the car. The Gwinnett County Police will meet us on Highway 20 and escort us toward the hospital until we meet the ambulance."

Stan had used the suction device to remove all the venom he could get out of Derrick's leg. "I got to get you in the car, buddy. You okay?"

"I feel like I'm going to pass out or puke."

Jasmine put her fingers on Derrick's wrist and looked at her watch. "Let me check your pulse real fast before he puts you in the car."

Twenty seconds later: "Your pulse feels weak, and your heart rate's down to about 48 beats-per-minute."

"Watch out darling," Stan said. She moved away and he reached down and picked him up, and then put him in the back of the CR-V.

Veronica blinked her lights when she saw the police escort sitting alone on the side of the road with blue lights flashing. The tires on the cruiser squealed when he pulled out in front of her to lead with the siren blaring, as he hurried them to meet the ambulance that waited in a parking lot near Interstate 985, several miles away. Derrick had called his mom after Stan had put him in the CR-V. Mrs. McCormick then contacted the Police Department to let them know it was her son whom had been bitten. Almost a half an hour later, she met them in the Emergency Room of the Gwinnett General Hospital, which was close to the shopping mall she was shopping at when Derrick called. Before they arrived, she had taken care of the primary paperwork. When she saw him come in through the double doors on the stretcher, she rushed over and said, "How's my baby boy?"

He raised his head. "My leg hurts and I feel kind of sick, Mom, but I think I'm okay."

"You look pale," she said, as she hastened along beside him on the stretcher.

An accompanying EMT from the ambulance said, "He'll be fine, Mayor McCormick. The other gentleman removed most of the venom with the snake bite kit before we got to him. If not for that, he may be in worse shape than what he's in, now. We just need to get him in there to get the antivenin, so please excuse us. He'll be ready to go real soon," he said.

"I'm okay. I'll see you shortly," Derrick said.

A tall and slender, dark-skinned, nurse stood with a clipboard by the admittance desk. "Roll him into Room B," she said. "The doctor will be right behind you." She looked at Mrs. McCormick and smiled. "You'll get my vote, again, Mayor McCormick. Your support here has made a big difference in our community. I'll see you at the next banquet," she said, before turning to rush down the corridor.

"I'm happy to serve you and the community, Trisha," Mrs. McCormick said. They knew each other from Town Hall Meetings.

Stan, Jasmine, and Veronica walked through the doors to greet her. Stan quickened his pace to give her a hug. "Hey, how's he doing?" he asked as he wrapped his arms around her.

"Everyone says he's okay, but you know me. I'm going to worry until he's back home and not looking so darn pale. He looks like a ghost. They're giving him the antivenin now."

"That's good. He's a tough guy. He'll come out better than before," he said, and then smiled.

Jasmine and Veronica came to where they stood.

Mrs. McCormick eyed Veronica for a second, but then smiled and spoke. "How are you two young ladies doing today?"

"We're fine," Jasmine said.

"Is he still okay?" Veronica asked.

"I believe so, but as I was telling Stanley, I'll feel better when he's back at home."

"He's going to be fine. Don't you worry," Stan said.

Mrs. McCormick put her arm around his shoulder. "The EMT told me that he would probably be in worse shape if you hadn't gotten that poison out. I thank you for that. And you, Veronica, please let your dad know how grateful I am to him for having put that snake bite kit in your car. I admire those with foresight. It's a trait we'd all benefit from if we had it. Maybe I'll give him some business next time something ails me," she said, her lips down-turned for a second. "At my pace, that's liable to be at any minute, with the way I'm constantly running around town trying to take care of one problem or another. I know the stress can't be good for me."

Veronica touched her arm. "I'll be sure to tell him as soon as I call. I know hearing it will make him happy."

Mrs. McCormick's demeanor changed when Stan spoke.

"But, if it weren't for you taking care of my problem, I'd have had nowhere to have gone when Mom got arrested. I don't know what I'd have done without you," he said, and then gave her another hug.

"You're too sweet, Stanley. It's my pleasure to have you around. I know Derrick really enjoys you being there, too. You're like the brother he wished he had."

"I've gotten attached to y'all, too," he said. "Staying there has changed me by showing me a way of life I probably wouldn't have ever seen if you hadn't invited me and Wendy into your home."

Before turning to walk toward the Nurses' Desk, Veronica said, "Excuse me, please. I'm going to go check on Derrick."

Jasmine walked up beside Stan and slid her arm around his waist. "Am I disturbing anything?" she asked.

"Nothing at all," Stan said. "I was telling her how much I appreciate all she has done for me."

A few minutes later, Mrs. McCormick excused herself for a bathroom break. Stan and Jasmine held hands as they walked to find a seat in the crowded Waiting Room. Three people in the corner got up to go meet someone coming in the door.

"Over there in the corner is a spot," she said. They quickened their pace to sit down before someone else did. Jasmine squeezed his hand. "Are you going to tell her?"

"Not right now, baby. She has enough on her mind. We have plenty of time for that."

"Did you really mean it?"

"Of course, I did, baby. Why else would I have asked you?"

"I don't know. … I guess I'm just worried about being so young and having this baby."

He gently placed his hands behind her head and pulled her face close to his. "Sweetheart, I want to get Mom's approval before we do. I don't have to, but I don't want to run off and just get married without letting her know. We'll set a date and be married right after that, all right? I love you, baby." He leaned over to hug her and then kissed the side of her neck.

"I love you, too. I'm just scared. That's all. I don't know how my dad's going to act about me getting pregnant. Mom won't be too concerned, I don't guess, because the same thing happened to her. She got pregnant with Belinda before her first marriage."

"I know you're worried but don't be. I promise you we'll marry real soon and handle whatever comes our way. Everyone will be happy for us, darling, so please stop worrying, okay?"

She stood and pressed the side of his head against her stomach. "Just think, a little Stanley might be in there."

He kissed her on the navel. "Might be a little Jasmine."

"It won't be long before we find out if it will be a boy or a girl or both. I'll go to the doctor in two weeks and she should be able to tell by then."

"I reckon we'll start picking names after that, huh? Doesn't your dad have you on his insurance policy?"

"Yeah, he does. I use it every time I go to the gynecologist."

"I'm glad of that. At least we won't have to worry about getting you a room in the hospital when it's time. I could get insurance for us, but I don't think they'd cover the pregnancy because you're already pregnant. I've heard people talking about them not wanting to pay for pre-existing conditions, and things like that, you know. ... I don't like insurance companies. Momma says they're a bunch of crooks."

Veronica saw them sitting in the corner and rushed over. "Where's Derrick's mother?"

"She's in the bathroom," Stan said. "Why? What's wrong?" He knew something wasn't right.

"I was talking with the nurse and overheard two doctors talking about a patient almost being in shock. I think they were talking about Derrick."

"Are you sure?" he asked.

"I'm sure that's what they were talking about, but when I asked if it was Derrick, one of them told me he couldn't give me medical information about someone else," she said in a sarcastic tone as she placed her hands on the sides of her hips. "And then both of them walked off without saying anything else.

61

The nurse wouldn't tell me, either. His Mother might be able to find out if it's him."

"She probably can since she's his mother and legal guardian," Stan said. "She should be out--"

Jasmine pointed toward the east hall. "There she is," she said.

Stan stood and waved to get her attention to let her know where they were seated. After Veronica repeated what she had heard, Mrs. McCormick went to the Nurses' Desk. Trisha had returned.

"Trisha, could you please do me a favor and go find out how my son is doing."

"I have his chart right here," she said. "His blood pressure dropped real low and he started having difficulty breathing a little earlier, so the doctor gave him some intravenous medications primarily used for allergic reactions. And, it says here that he gave him something for the blood pressure and a couple of puffs from an inhaler for his breathing." She flipped the page. "And that he seems to be responding well to the medications. But, he wants to keep him another hour for observation before releasing him. ... And that's about it," she said before closing his chart.

"Well, then I guess I don't have anything to worry about. Thanks for letting me know."

"You're welcome. Just have a seat and relax, Mayor McCormick. Everything is going to be just fine. I'll make sure your son gets the best of care available," she said and then smiled. "It won't be long and you can carry him home with you."

"STAT, Room D, Code Blue," came over the intercom.

Trisha grasped Mrs. McCormick's hand to shake before she turned to leave. "Gotta run. I hope to see you again real soon but under better circumstances," she said, then she smiled and rushed down the hallway.

"Maybe we can have coffee together one day," she said, thinking that Trisha could help her collect more votes from the African-American community.

"That'd be great," she said over her shoulder. "Leave a message at the desk when you have time to meet."

"Will do," she said and then went to tell the others what she had learned.

After the doctor cleared Derrick to leave, he left with his mother. Veronica carried Stan and Jasmine back to her parent's cabin for Stan to get Derrick's Viper, and for Jasmine to get her Z4. Stan followed her to her apartment to make sure she made it home safely. He wanted to stay but had to get the Viper home.

The next week Derrick introduced him to Clarence, a wired informant who lured him into carrying him to meet his connection.

Stan drove him in his Dodge Durango to meet Rhonda. Once inside, he said, "She can get you what you want."

A few minutes later, Clarence said what he wanted. "I need someone who can hook me up with large quantities of pills and a couple 0 Zs of meth every week. If you can arrange that, all of us can make enough cash within six months to buy a yacht," he said. "I've got people with big bucks backing me. Can you handle what I need?"

"Oh, I can handle all of that and more. The problem is that I don't want to meet any new people. I wouldn't be talking with you if I didn't trust him," she said, pointing at Stan.

After they left her house, Stan had no further involvement in their dealings.

Three federal DEA agents had sat in a van parked on the street behind her house and listened to their conversation. Another agent had filmed Stan and Clarence walking into and leaving her house. That led to the indictment in the federal drug conspiracy case that landed Stan in prison.

Mr. D

CHAPTER 9 – Jake

♦♦♦♦♦

"Let's go," he said, as he grabbed her right arm to pull her from his truck.

Before forcing her to come with him, he had wadded a ragged bandana and stuck it in her mouth to silence her screams. "I'll slice your throat if you take it out, you understand?" he had said.

Lights flickered through the windows from passing cars as he made his way to where he would rape her. He made her sit close to him so he could grope her budding breasts and make her fondle him. After he pulled into the roadside park, he got her out of the truck and led her into the forest. She was only twelve-years-old, his niece.

"I'm going to pull this out. If you scream or try to get away, you know what I'm going to do to you, don't you?"

She nodded. He removed the bandana and bent down to kiss her; his breath reeked of nicotine and alcohol.

She turned her head. "Please don't Uncle Jake."

He leaned down and whispered in her ear. "You listen here, Marsha. This won't hurt you. You just can't tell anyone, okay?"

She began to whimper. "No. Let go of me, Uncle Jake. Just take me home. I won't tell."

He grabbed her by the hair and pulled her head back to make her face him. Saliva dripped from his mouth. She wrinkled her nose and turned her head. "You better listen to me, little girl. Look at me," he said, then jerked her hair; put his face close to hers. "Stop that crying."

She glared at him, held her breath. Her eyes and cheeks were red, a stream of tears rolled down her face.

"If you tell anyone, I'll kill your Momma and Daddy. You understand?"

She nodded. More tears flowed as she sobbed.

"Now, shut up," he said. Then he covered her mouth with his. When she resisted and bit his tongue, he drew back and slapped her, then shoved her to the ground; lowered himself on top of her fragile little body.

"Help me," she screamed. "Help!"

"I warned you, you little bitch." He wrapped his hands around her throat and squeezed until she stopped fighting. Then he ripped off her clothes before rolling her over on her stomach. She had stopped breathing.

Ten minutes later, her limp body lay in the leaves below the sycamore trees.

He kissed the back of her neck and stood to zip his blue jeans. Damn, he thought, what the hell have I done? His heart pounded his ribs and sweat ran down his face and neck to his chest. I've screwed up real bad. God damn it, Marsha. Look what you made me do. His eyes darted to the horizon. I can't hardly see anything. If it wasn't for that street lamp I couldn't see shit. Over there's a place.

He dragged her by her feet to the edge of a bank and hid her in some underbrush before leaving.

Over the next two days, he helped his brother and the locals search for her, going door-to-door, and forming search parties. In the mountainous terrain where he had hid her, he knew no one would find her. He had her stashed in the bushes three counties away. At night he'd go back to her until the stench of rotting flesh kept him from having her again. Then he buried her in a shallow grave and went on to find four more victims during the next five-months, before law enforcement officials sent him to prison on an unrelated charge.

He sat in his truck and watched an older lady get out of a van to let her terrier go for a walk on a nature trail in the Blue Ridge Mountains, near one of the Civil War battle grounds. For the last half hour, he had sat smoking cigarettes and nursing a beer while he waited for someone to pull in to the roadside park.

"Here comes one," he mumbled, when he saw her slow to pull off the main road.

After she had stopped and sat for a moment, she glanced his way. He averted his gaze to look at the dashboard. She opened the door and climbed out with the small terrier in her arms.

Nice legs. I hope she doesn't get spooked. Clothes look expensive. New van. Maybe she's got some diamonds or gold. I might have some fun with her, even though she is older than I like. Come on granny. There you go. Go on down that trail.

He checked for traffic on the winding road leading to the site. Satisfied no one else was coming, he opened the door, took in a deep breath of mountain air, and then followed her into the woods.

Ruff ... Ruff, ruff, ruff.

"Shh, Fee Fee. That nice man's not going to bother us."

He saw her watching him coming down the trail, his hands in his pockets. "Hey, how you doing, young lady?" he said. He wanted to get closer to her to make his move. The dog continued to bark.

"Shh! Fee Fee, I told you he was nice," she said, and then brushed away a wisp of gray hair from her aged face. Her lips were upturned, her face a rosy red; flattered by his compliment. Fee Fee kept barking. "I'm doing well," she said. "Just trying to stretch my legs and let my baby relieve himself." She bent down toward Fee Fee. "Hush, now. Mamma's fine." Then she turned toward Jake, who was ten feet away. "This is my personal protector," she said, and then giggled.

"Ha, Ha, Ha," he said. I've got this bitch now, he thought. That dog's getting on my nerves. I can't wait to break its little neck. "Those are nice to have around. I have a Yorkshire," he lied. He removed his hands from his pockets.

"Are you from around here?" she asked, then stepped farther away from him. Fee Fee growled.

He kicked some leaves; his face slick with sweat, adrenaline flooding his veins. "No, I'm from somewhere else." That dog is going to get more than he wants. "Where you from?" He shifted his eyes, checked the parking area, reached into his back pocket as he moved closer to her.

"Florida. I came to see this National Park." She turned away and slid her left thumb under the front of her brassiere strap.

He yanked a hawk-bill knife from his back pocket. "Give me all your money and jewelry, old lady, and there won't be any trouble. I'll slice you and that mutt into pieces if you don't."

She pressed the micro switch in the lining of her bra to activate the alarm, and then slid a small pistol from under her left breast. Two federal agents burst from the back of the van, guns drawn. Both agents dashed down the embankment with their pistols aimed and ready. The larger of the two shouted, "Drop the weapon. Get on the ground."

When she heard her backup, Agent Loraina spun around and dropped to a crouch, aimed the gun at his puny chest. "Drop the weapon or I'll shoot!"

He dropped the knife. "What the fuck is going on?" he said. Then he lay in the leaves; shook his scraggly hair from his face.

"A sting operation," she said. "We've been after you for months for a string of robberies on a federal reservation." Fee Fee pranced around him, barking.

"Good job, Loraina," the case agent said. "You, too, Fee Fee." He looked at him on the ground and laughed. Then he swatted at a mosquito and said, "Put the cuffs on him and let's get out of this mosquito den."

Four months later, he pled guilty to the armed robberies on a federal reservation.

Justice for Marsha and the other little girls, delayed. A year later, the federal marshals escorted him to the federal penitentiary in Leavenworth, Kansas.

PART III

CHAPTER 10 – Vengeance

Stan returned from Big Bobby's cell, still thinking about what had happened in the TV room. Later that evening, after him and Bobby had eaten chicken fried steak, green peas and carrots, and cornbread in the chow hall, he told Bobby, "I have to wash my clothes, bro." Then he stopped by his cell; grabbed his laundry bag; went down the tier to the Laundry Room and set his bag on top of the washing machine to wait for his turn; two other bags were before his. A few feet down the tier, two older men that he knew were leaning on the rail talking. "Hey, Jimmy, do me a favor, please."

"Yeah, man. What can I do for you?"

"Keep an eye on my clothes for a few minutes. I'm going to run around the corner to the TV room and see if anything good is coming on tonight. All right?"

"I gotcha covered, my man."

"Thanks," he said, and then strolled down the tier.

The TV room was empty when he walked in. It smelled like weed; someone had been in there and smoked a joint. He stood channel surfing when he glimpsed Jake's partner walking by the door, which made him feel uneasy.

Three minutes later, Jake and the doorman with the shank, rushed into the room with their eyes wide open, jaws clinched. Stan turned to face them. "You want more?" he said.

Jake pulled a metal pipe from under his shirt. "I'm going to bust you up for you and the big guy disrespecting me," he said, as he raised the pipe to strike. Then he swung.

With his movement as graceful as a crane's, Stan maneuvered himself to the center of the room to dodge the blow. Then he spun and kicked Jake in the side, knocking the breath out of him.

"Oh, fuck," he said, grabbing the ribs on his left side.

The doorman held the shank in the upright position. He stepped around Jake and lunged at Stan; swung for the stomach. Stan jumped backwards, dodged the strike, and then struck the doorman's jaw with a forward thrust. The heel of his hand connected with the forward point of the jaw. Pow! The jaw broke. He staggered for a second. The shank fell to the floor. Stan kicked him in the groin, and then when he doubled over, chopped him in the back of the neck. He fell face-forward.

Jake swung again. Stan turned a nanosecond before the pipe would have struck his head. He ducked and deflected the blow with his forearm; moved to the side, and then grabbed Jake's arm and brought him over his shoulder, threw him across the room. The pipe clanged to the floor. Stan ran over and kicked him in the face. Jake covered his mouth with his hand. Blood gushed from between his fingers "Please," he mumbled through his hand, his eyebrows raised. Then Stan kicked him in the opposite side. Jake grimaced and rolled over to grab his side.

"You piece of shit. If you ever come near me again with a weapon, I'll kill you," he said. Then he spit on him.

The doorman raised his head and rolled over.

Stan looked at him and said, "You, too." Then he strutted out of the TV room to go let Bobby know what had happened in case he got locked up.

♦♦♦♦♦

The doorman stood over the sink in Jake's cell and rinsed blood from the washcloth. Jake sat on the toilet. "Look up at me," the doorman said, limiting the movement of his jaw as he spoke. "You're face is screwed. There's no way you can get near the hacks and not get locked up. What are you going to do? You need to go to medical and get stitched up."

"Just get a needle and thread. Stitch up the biggest cut on my lip."

"What about your eyes? You can't hide them. You look like a popped-eyed raccoon. They're swollen bad."

"I know what I look like. I've looked in the damn mirror. Just get busy and fix me up," he said. Then he rubbed his ribs. "I think that son-of-a-bitch broke three or four ribs on each side. They hurt like a mother fucker. I can't hardly breathe without it hurting."

"Man, I don't know about stitching you up. ... I'll try but I'm not a doctor. I think I need to work on that gash right there," he said, and pointed below Jake's eye. "It looks worse than your lip. Where's the needle and thread?"

"Look in that little box on the top shelf of the locker, all the way back by the shampoo."

"My jaw is probably broken. It hurts like hell," he said as he rummaged through the locker. "I found it."

After he had threaded the needle and began stitching a large gash below Jake's right eye, a guard peered through the cell-door-window, and then opened the door. "Step out," she said.

The doorman turned and said, "What's the problem?"

"Both of you need to step out of the cell."

She stood by the door with her finger on the body alarm button of the Motorola two-way radio, as the doorman ambled out onto the tier. Jake got up from his seat on the toilet and turned to face her. She raised her eyebrows. "My God, what happened to you?"

"I slipped in the shower."

"Yeah, right. Tell that to the lieutenant," she said. Then she spoke into the mouthpiece of the radio, clipped to the shoulder strap of her uniform. "B-Lower to Lieutenant Garcia."

"Go for Garcia."

"I've got two with facial wounds in cell 161."

When Lieutenant Garcia arrived and saw the extent of the wounds, he called for assistance and then locked down the cellblock to do a cell-to-cell, upper body search to look for others with injuries. No one else had visible injuries.

He had sent Jake and the doorman to medical, where he took pictures of their wounds before they were treated for the injuries. And then, after an examination by the P.A. and treatment for their injuries, he sent them to the hole for an investigation. Neither Jake nor the doorman told what had happened, even though the lieutenant said he would review the security cameras to track where they had been. An hour later, Lieutenant Garcia sent four guards to put Stan in the hole for an investigation because the video showed him coming out of the TV room before the other two with the injuries. Two months later, all three were released from the hole. Jake and the doorman had to sign a waiver of responsibility in order to be released, stating that they were responsible for their own safety, that their lives were not in danger, and that the administration would not be held accountable should injury occur as the result of their being released to the compound.

Before the Lieutenant released Stan, he had the guards to bring him to the office for a discussion. The lieutenant, a wiry man wearing gold-rimmed spectacles, sat twirling his gray handlebar mustache when Stan walked in the door, his arms handcuffed behind his back.

"Have a seat Mr. Mason," he said, pointing at a beige folding chair beside the door.

"Yes, sir." The cuffs clanged against metal as he sat.

"I looked at your record and saw that you had some serious trouble when you began your sentence."

"Yes, sir. That was a long time ago."

"I know it had to have been you that messed up the worlds of those two hyenas. That is, unless they messed up each other, but if that was what had happened, then why would Duval have been doctoring up Stephens when Officer Calhoun opened the door? I'm just running this through my mind."

Stan sat shaking his right foot but didn't respond.

"I just don't know why you would have done that to them. Are you sure you don't want to enlighten me, Mr. Mason?"

"I don't have anything to say. It's your investigation, not mine."

"I can appreciate that. But, I had to ask as part of this investigation. What's going to happen if I let you out?"

"As far as I'm concerned, nothing, I hope. My wife, daughter, and sister are planning to come visit me real soon, and I don't plan on doing anything to mess that up. You've looked at my record. I haven't been into any trouble for a while. I'm trying to get out of this place so I can live a normal life. I assure you, if no one bothers me, I won't bother them, but I will defend myself against anyone."

"Yes, that I know. I also know you gave that pervert, oh excuse me, did I say that? That person, a new face. He probably had that coming. From an administrative point of view, though, I have to protect even those I don't think deserve to breath good air."

"I understand."

"Man-to-man, if I let you out, do you intend on causing any harm to either of them, or do I need to transfer you?"

"Lieutenant, all I want to do is to do my time and to get the hell out of this madhouse. I'm not trying to harm anyone. To answer your question, no, I don't plan on doing anything to either one if they don't try bothering me or my family, but I can't promise anything."

"Thank you. I appreciate your honesty," he said. Then he stared at some papers and tapped his pen on the desk for a few seconds. "Okay. That'll do it. I'll let you know in a day or so what I will do."

"All right."

"Gene. I'm through with him. You can carry him back." Two guards escorted Stan back to the cell. The one with the keys opened the bean-hole. "Cuff up," he said.

"This is bullshit," Oscar said, as he rolled out of the top-bunk. Then he backed up to the door and stuck his arms through the opening.

"You know the routine. It's protocol. I don't like it any more than you do, but rules are rules. If I don't follow them someone will tell on me and get me in trouble," he said. The cuffs clicked when he closed them on his wrist.

"Open 201," he said.

Stan walked in the cell.

"Close 201."

After the door closed, Stan stuck his arms through the bean-hole. The guard removed the handcuffs. Stan stepped away from the door for Oscar to have his removed. When the guards went down the hallway, Oscar looked at Stan and smiled. "Well, what's the deal?"

"I think he's going to let me out. He said he'd let me know in a couple of days."

"Maybe he will. I know you're tired of this bullshit over here," Oscar said. He began pacing the cell. "It sucks not getting out of this sorry-ass cell except for rec. An hour a day just don't get it, especially with them putting us in a damn dog cage when we do go out. I don't know why the hell they don't let us go out during the weekends, too."

"I don't reckon they want us to have too much fun, huh?"

"Oh, yeah. They know we are having a lovely time here in Club Fed. When I was doing state time, I had always heard that the feds paid minimum wage for working, had conjugal visits, and all sorts of things that aren't true."

"Is that right? This is my first time ever being locked up for anything, and I hope it's my last. Hell, I've got a family I need to be out there with."

"How much longer you got?"

"Less than two years, if I'm good," he said, and then laughed. "It's the last part that's the hardest, living in a world full of lunatics looking for trouble."

"Amen, brother. That dickhead that I beat down just walked up and pushed me. Thought I was someone else. I smashed him, good. I bet you he thinks before he does something like that again. Ha, ha, ha."

"He probably will. I just hope I don't have any more trouble out of Jake and his crew. If they fuck with me though, I'll do what I have to do. Next time I won't be nice."

"What you think will happen?"

Stan lay on his bed, put his hands behind his head and crossed his legs. "Who knows? All I can say is that I don't trust either one of them. Big Bobby used to always try talking me out of doing anything to Jake, but after I told him about those bastards double-teaming me, he didn't have a lot to say. It pissed him off that they came in there with the intention of doing the typical chain-gang hit, one with a pipe to knock me senseless, and the other one with a shank to finish me off."

"How about him, what do you think he'll do?"

"Well, that's a hard one to answer. Bobby's a great guy, a gentle giant, but I damn sure wouldn't want to get him pissed at me. Quite frankly, I don't see him doing anything to anyone unless they try doing something to him or someone he cares about. He's a real protective person. With me, though, he'd probably let me fend for myself," he said. Then he closed his eyes. "He knows I can handle myself. ... I'm going to rest my eyes for a little. We'll talk more later."

"I'm going to do some push-ups. You don't mind, do you?"

"Go right ahead; work it out, my friend."

The next day, the guard came to the door. "Pack it up, Mason. You're going to the compound."

Mr. D

CHAPTER 11 - Deceit

"Thanks," Stan said, as the SHU property officer handed him the two green duffel bags that contained all of his belongings accumulated over the last few years. He grabbed the side handles and lugged the bags across the compound. When he entered the main hallway, a Mexican prisoner met him at the door.

"Amigo, que pasa? Need help?"

Between breaths, he said, "I'd appreciate it, Jose." He sat down both bags to take a quick breather, and then handed him the lightest of the two.

"I get you to door," he said. Then he bent down and slid under the shoulder straps to tote it on his back.

Stan grabbed the other one by the strap and slung it over his shoulder. "That'll work. It's a long way to the unit from the hole. These things get heavy after a while."

"Si, me know."

A couple of minutes later, Jose handed him the bag in front of B-Lower.

"Mucho gracious, amigo," Stan said. He wasn't fluent in Spanish, but liked to show his Hispanic friends courtesy by using the few words he did know. The ones who weren't fluent in English did the same with him with their limited English. "That helped a lot. I'll see you around."

"No problem," he said, and then turned and waved before heading back up the hallway toward the chow hall.

Terry met him on the bottom tier as he turned the corner. He ran up to help him with the bags. "What's up, dude?" he said. "I've been wondering what they were going to do with you."

"I'll fill you in as soon as we get this junk in the cell," he said. "Where's Bobby?"

"I think he's working in the Print factory, right now. He should be in before long."

"Is anyone in 248? I ain't trying to move in with some idiot."

"It's still open, I believe. I don't think they put anyone in there."

"That's unusual."

"Yeah it is. Maybe someone looked out for you," Terry said. "It impressed people when you whipped both of them."

The cell was empty. After they put the bags down, a few seconds later, Stan shook hands with him and then said, "I got lucky. I thought they were going to transfer me, for a moment. The SHU Lieutenant wanted to know what would happen if he let me out, and I let him know straight up that I wasn't planning on doing anything, but would damn sure defend myself if anyone messed with me."

Terry reached down and picked up a tiny quartz-crystal on the floor that had come from an old watch. "I already talked with Jake and his partner. They say it's over, too. Jake's face looks a little different. What the hell did you do to him?"

"I ain't getting into all of that, but you can believe they don't want to tangle with me anymore," he said. Then he smiled. "I showed them a few of those moves I learned years ago."

"Yep, I guess you're right. They probably don't."

"Has Wendy mentioned when she's planning to come visit us?"

"Last week she said something about the Fourth of July weekend. She was going to call Jasmine to see if that would be a good time for her, because she knew you'd want to see Jessica."

"You're damn right, I do. That's my little princess. That's why I've got to stay out of all the stupid stuff, man. I gotta get out of here or I'll end up spending the rest of my life in here, like Bobby keeps telling me. I'll call in a few minutes and see what's on the agenda. Maybe they'll be able to make it. I know I'da been madder than hell if I had been found guilty and lost my visits."

"That would have really been bad."

"Jasmine would have kicked my ass when she found out," he said. Then he laughed. "It's just hard to let some things go. I don't think anyone blames me for what I did to either one of those idiots, and I damn sure hope nothing else comes of it, but y'all got to leave Wendy out of all your plans. You know what I mean?"

Terry looked out the cell-door-window. "Yeah, I know. I'll try to work something else out."

"You need to leave that stuff alone. Look at your arms. They look like pin cushions. If a cop were to see them, you'd probably get a U.A. or locked up."

He wiped his nose with his sleeve. "I know man. I can't stand one of them, right now. I'm trying to quit. You know I am."

"I don't reckon it's easy. ... I'll tell you this, though. You'll end up losing Wendy if you don't. She won't keep putting up with it. She loves you, I know, but I know she doesn't like the thought of you killing yourself by shooting all of that tar and cocaine."

He continued looking out the window for a minute, and then said, "I need to go see someone. I'll see you a little later. Let me know what you find out about the visit. I can't call until I get some more phone minutes. All right?"

"All right. I'll let her know you love her."

"I appreciate it. Later," he said and then went back to his cell on the other side of the cellblock. Five minutes later, he and his cellmate sat drinking Tang. Jake knocked on the door. "Come on in," Terry said. "I sure hope the doctor's in town. I feel like someone's inside twisting my guts."

"Damn right, he's at your door," he said. He came in and leaned against the wall, started fumbling around in the front pocket of his trousers. "It's the bomb.

This time it's China White. Not tar." He pulled out a sandwich bag with several corners of plastic bags, twisted and sealed with clear tape.

Terry stood gazing.

His celly frowned. "I'm going to take a walk while you do your thing. Excuse me," he said. "I'll yell Hey Peckerwood if I see the hack heading this way."

Jake moved out of the doorway so he could leave. "What's up with that? You think everything's okay?"

"Yeah, it's cool. He just don't like watching me shoot up."

Jake pulled the door almost closed, and then held open the bag. "Here, take your pick. Some's a little bigger than the others."

"Let me get three for a hundred. Can you stand it?"

"All I need to know is when you can pay. I know your money's good."

"I'll call and have Wendy to wire the money just as soon as I get more phone minutes, next week. She'll do it. I could ask Stan to call for me, but you know what the deal is there."

"Cool. Get you three good ones. What did he have to say about me?" he said, and then stepped closer. "You think I need to watch him?"

"He said it's over as long as y'all don't try anything. He's not looking for trouble, but he still don't want me to get my ole lady involved in anything."

"Where you at with that?"

"Look here, dude. My ole lady's coming to see me before long," he said. "If I can make two grand by getting her to bring me a little package, what do you think I'm going to do?"

Jake smiled. "We'll talk. Take care of yourself now."

Terry reached in his waistband and took out a binky he had made by melting an insulin needle into a pinky finger-size piece of plastic tubing. He used a rubber

82

band to connect a short piece of milk tube to the opposite end. Sweat dripped from his chin. After he mixed the China White on top of a torn piece of aluminum from a soda can, he put the heat to it with a lighter smuggled in by a guard on the take. Then he squeezed the binky to pull the mixture through some cotton from a cotton swab. "It broke down clean," he said.

"That's good. You're going to like it, I guarantee that," Jake said. He peeked out the door. "All's well. I don't see anything. Just a few lames moving around."

Terry sat on the toilet, tied his left arm with a boot lace as he gently held the end of the binky between his teeth. He bit on the plastic to keep the pressure from pushing any of the heroin out. He pumped his fist to raise the veins, and then he jabbed the point into the one that raised the highest. When he felt the sting, he thought of a lyric from "She Talks to Angels" by the Black Crows. Seconds later, he closed his eyes to enjoy the chemical-induced tranquility that coursed through his body. Thirty seconds later the porcelain god demanded it's due. He puked. He puked some more. He ran out of fluid to throw up and then gagged with the dry-heaves.

Jake shook his head. "Is it getting good to you, yet?"

Terry turned his head and wiped the vomit from his lips with some toilet tissue. The pupils in his eyes were pinned. "Maybe I shouldn't have did the whole bag."

"I told you it was the bomb. Your eyes are bloodshot."

"Hell, what do you expect? I've done puked my guts out."

Jake sat on the edge of Terry's bed. "So, what you want to do about the package? Do you think you could talk her into bringing it in, if I had someone to drop off an ounce of good stuff?"

"It's a good possibility. If nothing else, she has a wild ass girlfriend who might bring it in to someone for me. I don't really think Nicole likes me, but she likes money. She might want to buy some more titties. She already spent a fortune on breast implants."

83

Terry's celly returned. "You look like shit," he said.

"I'm happier than a punk with two assholes now that I have some medicine in me," Terry said.

Jake grinned. "You should have heard him barking at the moon a few minutes ago."

"I puked so much I thought my stomach came out. It's some good stuff, though. I just did a little more than I needed."

His celly took off his shoes, placed them under the bed, and then climbed the ladder to get in the top bunk. "I'm going to read a little."

After a while, Jake and Terry forgot he was up there. They continued talking. Before Jake left out of the cell, he said, "I gotta go and see if I can round up more business. When do you think you will know if she will move something for us?"

"Next time I call I'll try to feel her out, but with the calls being recorded, I can't say anything over the phone, so it will be when she comes to visit before I will know for sure."

"That'll work. Hell, see if her girlfriend wants to come visit me. That would be great. We just need to come up with a plan to keep your brother-in-law out of our business."

"Maybe he'll croak or something. I get tired of him always--."

"Fuck him. I think about him every time I look in the mirror. He's a tough guy, all right, but if I catch him sleeping ... I'll--."

"Hold up, dude, keep that to yourself. All right? I don't need to know anything like that. He'd kill me if he found out I knew and didn't say anything."

"That's cool. I need to cruise," Jake said, and then left the cell.

Terry's celly lay in the bed facing the wall, thinking.

When the noise level increased by the factory workers returning from work, Stan went to wait at the door leading into the cellblock. Several men stopped by to shake hands and said things like, "If you need anything let me know," or "Yell at me later if you need any help," or "That was some job you did on them," or "You got my respect."

Big Bobby strolled in the door and saw him standing against the wall. He ran over and gave him a hug. "Hi, Pal. How's it going?"

"Better now that I can move around and get some fresh air," he said, and then smiled.

"Where'd they put you? Back in the same cell?"

"Yeah, it surprised the hell out of me."

Both turned and walked toward the cells.

"I spoke up for you. The Unit Manager told me he'd hold it until the investigation was over."

"I appreciate it. I'll let you know what happened after the count."

"You need anything?"

"I'm good. I got all my property. From what I can tell, nothing's missing."

After the count, Stan explained all that had gone down since the last time they had spoken. Then they went to chow and ate roast beef, wheat bread, potatoes and gravy. Stan's friends in the other units did the same as those had done in the cellblock; offered assistance and congratulated him. A lot of people knew why Jake was in prison and did not like anyone who victimized older people. With prison being of a violent nature, Stan automatically gained more respect and admiration from his peers by defeating two men whom had weapons. When the ones who were defeated were not well liked anyway, it gave him even more than what would normally have been due.

Two weeks later, Stan and Bobby were walking the track when Terry's celly walked up beside them. "Hey, Stan, we need to rap."

"What's on your mind?"

"You want me to walk on?" Bobby said.

"You're all right," Terry's celly said. "All I've got to say is that your sorry ass brother-in-law is plotting with that scumbag to do some slimy shit you need to know about."

"I'll catch you next lap, bro," Stan said to Bobby. Then him and Terry's celly slowed their pace, while Bobby quickened his to get ahead of them.

Stan raised his eyebrows. "What's going on?"

"I hate getting involved with this, but I would want you to give me a heads up, if the situation was reversed. You know I don't care much for either of them."

"Can't blame you."

"The day you got out of the hole, the snake came by and sold him some dope. I got out of there while he did his thing. ... After he had shot it, I came back and crawled up in the bed to read. Let's go get some water."

"Okay. You're killing me, man. Get to the point, please."

They headed for the water fountain. "He's planning on doing something. I don't really know what. If I were you, I wouldn't let him sneak up on me. He's still pissed because you kicked his ass. He's--."

"If he messes with me again, I'll kick the bastard to sleep and send him to meet his maker. Should of did it last time."

"That's not all, but I'm skeptical about telling you this."

"Don't worry about it. I want to know anything that's going on where me and my family is concerned."

"That's what concerns me. It's about your family," he said, and then stopped to gulp some water.

Stan stood with his hands on his sides, sweat running down his face. "Now you really have me interested."

"You have a visit coming in a couple of weeks or so?"

"Supposed to."

"They were talking about having your sister to bring something next time she--."

"You've got to be joking. I've warned both of them already. If he tries that bullshit, I'm going to rearrange his face, too."

"That's why I didn't want to be involved. I'm not trying to get caught in the middle."

Stan took a drink of water, wiped his mouth with the back of his hand, and then said, "Don't let this go any further, all right?"

After they were back on the track, Stan said, "You did the right thing. Now I have to do what I should have done months ago. It makes me mad as hell that both of them ignored what I told them about not involving Wendy in their plans. I guess they think I'm some kind of a punk or something." His face turned red as he picked up his pace, slinging his arms in a forward/backward motion as he strutted along the track. "And I'm damn sure not going to walk around wondering if that piece of shit is going to cop a sneak on me. Make sure you keep quiet."

"I won't mention anything to anyone."

"Thanks," Stan said. He shook hands with him and then rushed to catch Bobby. Afterward, he didn't go into detail about what he had learned. He wanted to think it over, and with what he was thinking, he knew Bobby would try talking him out of doing it.

He thought it over. Jake had to go.

CHAPTER 12 – Mercy

"Don't do it, bro," Bobby said. "It's not that serious."

Stan handed him the duct tape after taping the boot lace to the handle. "Here, hold this," he said, "so I can get busy. I'm tired of worrying if he's going to sneak up and stick me."

"You know he's more mouth than anything."

"I can't take a chance at being wrong."

"Brother, I know you better than that. You're not scared of him or afraid he'll try anything. It's about Wendy, isn't it?"

"I won't lie. That has a lot to do with it. I told him in the TV room that day to leave her out of their plans."

"Why don't you wait and see how you feel about it tomorrow?"

"I'll feel the same way. When I was in the chow hall, I saw him whispering to his buddies and pointing at me. No one's going to talk about doing something to me and get away with it," he said. He checked the drop of the shank and it fell into the palm of his hand.

"That'll do it. It's time to ride. If something happens and I don't come back, call Wendy and have her to let Jasmine know not to come visit. They'll be so angry with me that I wouldn't want to see--."

"You know I will do whatever you need," he said. Then he crossed his arms. "I give up trying to get you to let it go." He ducked his head and stepped out onto the tier, then he hesitated a moment before he turned and said, "Good luck, pal," and went back to his cell.

◆◆◆◆◆

Jake sat on the toilet in the rear of the cell. He leaned over and refined the point of the blade by scraping it against the concrete seam at the base of the wall.

Two minutes later, he checked the point with his fingertip. A quick stab in the spine will do just fine, he whispered to himself. He snickered as he stood and slid the shank in a cardboard sheath. He squeezed the handle and prayed a prayer he once heard someone say who was into the dark spirits: "Ashes to ashes, dust to dust, God won't have him, so the Devil must." Then he slid the sheath in the back of his trousers, above the right side of his hip.

He caught a glimpse of himself in the mirror, rubbed the scar below his eyes where Stan had kicked him. That son-of-a-bitch, he thought. "I'll show him who the tough guy is when I drive this mother fucker into his stinking-ass heart. He thinks he can do me anyway he wants because he knows that kung-fu junk. I'll show him," he mumbled as he combed his hair back toward the crown. He touched his hair, smiled, and then he turned and walked out of the cell. After looking both ways, he went back inside to the toilet to relieve the pressure. It'd be terrible to piss in my pants when I'm killing that bastard, he thought. He relaxed to let it go. The water spattered.

◆◆◆◆◆

Stan stepped to the door, surprised that it was open. He stood and smiled for a second when he looked and saw Jake taking a piss with his back turned to him. He let the shank fall into place as he fought the impulse to run into the cell and start stabbing him in the kidney. He'd rather watch the surprise in Jake's eyes when he turned and the blade struck below the sternum. He crept toward his prey. It would be over with one upward thrust and a quick twist of the blade to leave a gap wide enough for the life to leak out onto the floor. Jake's chance of survival was about as good as an ice cube's chance of not melting on a hot plate on high heat. He edged closer, moving on the sides of his shoes to not make a sound and to avoid detection. One more step, his prey three feet away.

He clutched the handle: shank facing forward, his palms sweating, mind speeding, stress soaring. Tension. Heart pounding. Adrenaline scorching veins. Fighting hate, wrestling reason, and then Bobby's voice resonated from deep within; bombarding his mind with data; the words rang true, "Let it go, it's not that serious." An image of Jasmine and Jessica flashed in his mind. He stopped. "Hey, man, we gotta talk."

Jake jumped, splattered the wall, and stopped midstream. "You've got my undivided attention, Stan-tha-man." He adjusted himself and began buttoning his pants.

Stan slid the shank back up his sleeve. "You got a problem with me you want to talk about?"

"You know what the deal is. That shit in the T.V. room before we got locked up and you getting in my--."

"You and your partner asked for it, man. I had warned you a long time ago. Told you and that idiot that y'all had to leave my sister out of your plans or we'd have trouble."

Jake turned to face him, put his hands on his hips.

Stan watched, thought about letting the shank fall into place. "Don't try it. I know you're strapped. I saw--"

"I don't appreciate you coming in here disrespecting me, like that."

"I didn't come to talk, and we wouldn't be talking now if I wasn't trying to get out of prison."

Jake turned and looked in the mirror, wiped the sweat from his forehead with his right hand. "I want to get out, too," he said, and then turned on the faucet to wash his hands.

Stan stepped backward, toward the door. "We can go to war and get it over with right now if you want, but who will be the winner when one gets life and the other gets dead?"

He dried his hands on a green towel. Silence filled the room, except for the distant chatter of other prisoners. A few seconds later, he said, "You're right. We both lose no matter who walks away."

"Someone told me you were plotting on doing something to me and that's why I came in here the way I did."

91

Jake spun to face him. "Who the fuck said something like that?"

"You know I can't say."

"What would you be thinking if I'd fucked up your face?"

"Probably the same. It's over with, though, but from my perspective, I believe you had it coming. What would you have done if I had did to you what you and Duval tried to do to me?"

"Well, ... all right. Let's drop it, then. We can keep this between us. Is that cool with you?"

"Sure," he said. He reached out his hand at an upward angle to shake. Their palms met as they wrapped thumbs, then twisted for the typical handshake, and then grasped fingers before releasing their grip. Both of their lips were upturned when Stan left the cell and strolled down the tier, relieved of the pressure that had been driving him for days.

He walked up to Bobby's door and peeked in to see if he was in there. Their eyes locked. "I let it go," he said, and then walked on to his cell. Bobby burst in thirty seconds later, as excited as a puppy seeing its master return with Puppy Chow after a long trip. He grabbed him in a bear hug; lifted him into the air, squeezed, relieved that his partner was okay.

With a red face and veins popping out on his neck and forehead, Stan said, "Put me down, man, before I beat your ass."

"Ha, ha, ha. I'll break your back, Jack," he said, as he lowered him to the ground.

"Help me get this stuff off," he said. He raised his shirt and Bobby started pulling on the duct tape to remove the magazine armor. Stan slid the strap of the shank over his wrist. "I'm glad I didn't use this thing."

"I'm glad you didn't, too. What happened?"

"I had him, man. I walked up and caught him with his back turned and the door open."

Bobby yanked a piece of tape stuck to the skin.

"Ouch!" Stan said.

"Quit crying, Sissy. Tell me what happened," he said, as he removed the last section of the magazine armor. He tossed it in the garbage can.

"Thanks. Anyway, I walked right up on the stupid-ass. He was taking a piss with the door open. Man, I wanted to just run in and start stabbing the hell out of him. I don't really know why I didn't, other than wanting to watch the fear in his eyes when I ran it under his ribs. Let me put this up," he said, and then fumbled with the mattress to hide the shank.

"Why didn't you do it?"

"I came real close. I eased right into the cell with all intent of putting his lights out, but then I heard your voice as if you were in there with me." He turned away to face the rear of the cell, filled with emotion. Tears welled in his eyes. "I heard you say what you did before I went down there. ... Let it go, it's not that serious, is what I heard."

"That's good. I didn't think you were listening."

"Man, I was within three feet of him. I was drenched in sweat, ready to take him out, and then I just stopped, cold. All sorts of stuff was running through my head. When I stopped, he was still pissing and I told him we needed to talk."

"That's a hell of a note, ain't it," he said, and then chuckled. "Caught him with his back turned and walked right up on him, huh? That reminds me of something a Native American told me. Something like Counting the Coup. It's when they have a chance to kill someone and then give them a pass. You know, show them mercy. Maybe even touch the enemy with a stick to let them know they could have killed or harmed them." His eyes beamed as he smiled. "I'm glad it turned out the way it did."

Stan shook his head. "I don't know. Part of me says I did the right thing, and another part says I should have went ahead and killed him, or to at least stuck him a few times to get him off the compound."

"Well, I don't see how it would have helped you if you had done that. You know you would have gotten caught and picked up another case."

"I just don't trust him, Bobby."

Shortly afterward, Stan moved the shank out of his cell, hoping he wouldn't need it again.

CHAPTER 13 – Karma

"What are you doing here, Stan," she said.

"I might ask the same of you, Officer Calhoun."

"You first."

"Remember Rhonda? The short blonde who hung out with Henry, Derrick's friend?"

"Yeah, the one with the weed and stuff."

"Yep, that's her. Well, Henry introduced me to this guy named Clarence, who turned out to be a wired informant. He got all of us busted on a drug case. I'm doing ten years for just carrying him over to meet her. That's it. Nothing else. Can you believe that?"

Veronica nodded her head. "I'm studying criminal justice and have learned a lot about conspiracy laws. Some say it's the most abused law ever created, while others praise it for helping to get some of the otherwise 'Untouchables' off the street," she said, using her fingers to make quotation marks for "Untouchables" as she spoke.

"I never thought I'd be in prison for such bullshit."

"You and thousands of others. The common person doesn't have a clue about how the law works or how easy it is to end up in prison. I want to help fight to change things. That's why I'm majoring in Criminal Justice. It's also why I am here in this silly uniform, trying to get some college credits." She stepped into his cell and whispered. "Don't let anyone know that you know me. They'll put you in the hole and transfer one of us, if you do. You know, they're afraid of us getting put in a compromised position by one of you convicts," she said, before kissing him on the cheek and turning to leave. "I'll get back with you."

"Later, then. We'll talk some more when we can. I won't put you on the spot, okay."

She waved and then closed his door before she walked down the tier.

He lay back on his bed and thought about how wild life was, at times. He never imagined that he would see someone he knew from Georgia, in Leavenworth, Kansas; especially, her, working as a prison guard. Derrick had done her wrong by cheating on her. Maybe he'd call and let him know he had seen her. Then again, that wasn't a good idea with the phone calls being recorded. Next week when Jasmine comes to visit, I'll have her to let him know, he thought before he closed his eyes to rest.

The next morning Bobby stopped by to see how he was doing. "What's up, bro?" he said.

"Not a lot. S.O.S., you know the routine."

"Unfortunately, I know it too darn well," Bobby said. He ducked to enter the cell and then propped against the wall.

Stan sat up on the bed. "What you have planned for the day?"

"I don't know. Not much. With it raining as hard as it is, I doubt if they will open the yard anytime soon. I think there may be a tornado watch for the area until this afternoon."

"After we go eat breakfast, maybe we can play a few hands of knock gin."

"That's a bet. I'll let you get ready," he said, and then he ducked to leave. "See ya later."

A few minutes later they were in the chow hall eating bran flakes and pastries with milk and coffee. Other prisoners chattered, joked, plotted, and schemed on ways to get away with their dirty deeds; some thought and spoke of ways to improve themselves to increase their chances of not returning to prison when released, that is, those who will be released. Outside, lightening flashed through the rolling gray clouds; thunder boomed, vibrated walls; rain beat the plains and soaked the wheat and corn fields. Life happened.

Back in the cellblock, Jake sat drinking moonshine, distilled by cooking off homemade wine that the makers called Hooch or Buck, which they made from any variety of fruit, sugar, and yeast. Duval had gone to eat. If alcohol was available, Jake drank. He took a sip and then stood in front of the mirror, rubbed the scar from Stan's foot, then he slightly staggered out of the cell to roam the cellblock.

♦♦♦♦♦

An hour later, Stan and Bobby were in Stan's cell. Bobby sat on a makeshift stool, picking the tiny balled-up pieces of wool from the army blanket draped across Stan's bed, while Stan sat on the bed with a deck of cards in front of him, preoccupied with thoughts about the incident with Jake.

"Are you going to play cards or what?"

The sound of Bobby's voice snapped him back into the moment. He glanced at his partner and smiled. "Man, I'm glad I didn't kill that bastard. You saved me, brother, by talking some sense into my head, and I want you to know that I appreciate what you did. Thank--."

"Yeah, yeah, yeah, deal the cards," Bobby said, before the smile escaped that he had tried holding back.

"All right, I get the point." He picked up the deck and began shuffling. They played knock gin until the 10:00 A.M. count, and then went to brunch, as was their usual routine on Saturday morning. The wind and rain pounded the windows, while they walked down the tier to finish playing cards.

"That's some storm, isn't it? I ain't seen it rain that hard in a long time. The farmers are probably happy about it."

"Yep, probably so."

Back in the cell, Stan made himself a cup of bitter black coffee. "That wasn't much of an omelet, was it?"

"What omelet? What I had wasn't much more than eggs folded over, but, hey, at least they fed us, right?"

"Want a soda or coffee?"

"Soda, please. I've had enough coffee."

Stan put his coffee on the locker and then reached into the ice-filled-container that was once a five-gallon bucket of paint. "Here you go," he said, and handed him a Sprite. Then he picked up his coffee cup and sat with his back to the front wall. Facing the door, Bobby sat on an upturned garbage can; for comfort, he had a folded blanket on top of the can. Stan pushed him the cards. "Your deal."

The cards slapped against each other as Bobby shuffled them on the end of the bed. Stan sat in a trance replaying the events from the day he and Jake had agreed to peace. Something didn't seem right but he couldn't figure out what it was. Bobby dealt the cards, quickly sliding them from pile to pile. After dealing, he looked over at Stan. "What's going on inside that head of yours, pal? You look like you're in la la land or some forbidden place."

"Huh? What did you say?" The skin on his forehead bunched as his eyes narrowed.

"I asked what's going on with you. What's on your mind?"

Stan picked up a few cards, organized them by suit, and then froze for a few seconds before speaking. "You might think I'm crazy, but something ain't right, bro," he said. Then he started twisting his mustache.

"How you mean?"

"I'm getting some bad vibes but don't know why, or what's up, but I know something ain't right."

"That's strange," Bobby said. He sipped his soda, sat it on the floor, and wrinkled his forehead as he looked up.

"Why you say that?" He thought Bobby was insinuating that he was weird or not quite right in the head because of how he was feeling.

"Well, it's because I've been feeling uneasy, myself, but don't have a clue as to why." He shifted in his seat. "Might have something to do with us talking about Jake a little earlier."

"Maybe it's just paranoia. I don't--."

"Might be, but who knows. Play cards and forget about it. It's probably nothing."

Stan picked up the remainder of his cards; switched on his Walkman, adjusted his headphones to hang on the top bunk bed rail. Axel Rose screamed out the lyrics of "Welcome to the Jungle" through the headphone speakers. He turned it up, rocked to the beat for a moment, and then paused before he discarded a deuce of clubs.

Bobby picked up the discard, threw down an eight of hearts, and then he glanced up at the slot in the cell-door-window and saw Jake's face, peeking in the cell. "Watch out," Bobby said, a second before Jake yanked open the door and pulled a shank from the waistband of his khaki trousers. Bobby knocked over the garbage can with his leg when he jumped up. He stumbled backward a step before he regained his balance.

Jake rushed in with the shank in his right hand, held low, facing forward. A split-second later, he swung toward the left side of Stan's chest. Stan twisted toward him and averted the blow with a forearm block. Jake jerked away and recoiled for another strike. He grunted as he advanced. "You're mine, bitch!" he said, with words slurred, his face contorted and his eyes emitting rays of hate and rage. He lunged again, the shank in the upright position. He led with his knee to use his body weight in an attempt to pin Stan between the wall and bed, as he swung with a wide arc to strike him in the neck. Before the blade struck flesh, Stan blocked the blow with a green, vinyl-covered pillow. The point plunged into the fabric. Stan mumbled, "I'm killing you, punk," his voice strained under the pressure of keeping the shank at bay with the pillow between them. Jake pressed him against the wall, then said, "Mother fu--"

Bobby had coiled his massive right arm under Jake's chin and yanked. He had the palm of his hand at the base of his head. Jake reversed the shank's direction to take a backward swing at Bobby's torso, but his time to strike passed a nano-second before he could take the shot. Bobby used his right arm for leverage. With his other hand, he shoved the head forward with enough force to snap a tree limb. Then he raised to his full height and yanked him off the ground.

Jake's eyes bulged, his legs and feet twitched and dangled. Bobby backed up and slammed into the locker, knocked the bowl of assorted candies off onto the floor. He shook him by the neck as a lion or tiger might do its prey, before he let go and dropped him. Jake lay face-forward on the floor with the many different colored pieces of hard candy.

Stan jumped from the bed. "What the hell," he said, gasping for breath, his face as pale as a fresh cadaver in a morgue. A stream of sweat dripped into his left eye when he looked down at Jake, whose nose had trickled blood to form a crimson circle beside his head on the cold concrete.

"Relax, pal," Bobby said. He narrowed his eyes as he rubbed his chin. "Well, that's one problem solved. That one won't cause anyone trouble anymore."

Stan's pupils were as large as red grapes. "I didn't know what the hell was going on for a few seconds," he said, gazing at Bobby, whose eyes were riveted on Jake's listless body.

Bobby used the toe of his boot to roll him over on his back. "What a waste of good air, he was. He just couldn't honor the peace accord. Look what it got him: dead. I have--"

"I told you something wasn't right," Stan said, then wiped the sweat from his forehead.

"Yeah, you did. Sad that it had to happen, but at least you don't have to worry about him again." He folded his arms across his chest. "You know, I've seen a lot of 'em die because of anger after drinking that Liquid Courage. It's instant stupidity for some, like him."

Saliva oozed from the corner of Stan's mouth. "I should stomp his fuckin' face, man." He wiped his mouth with the back of his right hand, stared down at Jake, and then began twisting the tip of his mustache.

Bobby stood silent.

The tension from Stan's face slowly abated. "I reckon we need to get the guards to haul this piece of shit out of here."

Bobby stared at Jake a few seconds before responding.

"Prepare for questioning is what we need to do right now," he said. He turned and went to the sink; splashed water on his face, and then cupped his hands to catch some water, sipped some, and then used his shirttail to dry his face and hands.

"What should we say?" he asked. While Bobby was at the sink, Stan straddled Jake's body to stand with his back to the door, blocking the view from the cell-door-window, in case a gawker walked by looking in cells. Four men in the common area had been shouting and banging bones on the table as they played Dominos, so he was confident no one had heard what had went on, but he wasn't sure anyone had seen Jake enter the cell. The cameras could only have him walking into the cell, but probably not pulling the shank. He didn't remember where Jake was standing when he pulled it out and started trying to stab him.

Bobby turned back around to face him. "We can mostly tell the truth. Just don't need to mention anything about Wendy or Terry. No need to involve them, but you might not want to say anything, since it may get referred for outside prosecution. Ask for a lawyer first, if that's what you want to do, but I really don't know if that's what you should do."

"All right. I probably won't. Hell, the son-of-a-bitch came in here and tried to stab me, man. I don't see where I have anything to hide, as far as the actual murder goes."

The cell began to reek of urine and feces from Jake's organs expelling their content. Stan squinched his nose.

"Damn, it stinks in here. Let's get out of here."

"Okay, but we need to get the story straight."

Stan frowned. "All right," he said, and then paused. "I'll say he ran in here drunk as hell and tried to stab me first, but then turned and tried to stab you. And then, uh, after taking a swing at you, then he turned back to stab me, and that's when you grabbed him by the neck. And, uhh, you know, when you accidentally fell on him and broke his sorry-ass neck. How does that sound?"

"Too many theatrics pal. Just tell the truth about me grabbing him. I'm going to confess about what I did. He had a weapon and he did try to stab me. I just broke his neck before he could stick me."

"All right. I'll leave off the part about you falling on him. I'll say I don't recall everything. I was in shock."

"That sounds good to me. It will be a while before we see each other again. They'll separate us during the investigation of his death."

"Call or write Jasmine or Wendy when you can. Either one will let me know what you said."

"Whatever happens with this, I want you to know that you did the proper thing by going to him in peace. He chose his fate." Bobby shook his head as he looked at Jake's body. "What a shame. Just a damn kid. Too bad he had to die in a place like this."

"He got what he deserved, in my opinion."

"I'm sure you're right. Karma always gets its due. No telling what he did to deserve such an end. Maybe nothing."

"Yeah, but...." He reached out and shook hands and gave him a hug. "Let's take care of it," he said. Then they went to see the guard and let him know a dead body was in the cell.

The guard called for assistance, which flooded the cellblock with prison officials, whom began shouting, "Lockdown, all prisoners to their cells," a minute before they started locking the cell doors.

The guards cuffed and escorted Stan and Bobby to the Lieutenant's Office. He called them in one at a time to ask what they had to say. Both said what they had planned, and then the lieutenant had them escorted to the hole.

PART IV

CHAPTER 14 – Freedom

♦♦♦♦♦

Two years later, Stan lived in Georgia with Jasmine and Jessica. He went to visit his sister when he could.

On a sunny Saturday morning, in the front yard of Wendy's ranch-style home, a mocking bird perched on the branch of a Dogwood tree and sang a cheerful song. Stan sat in an avocado green recliner, reading the USA TODAY newspaper, his feet propped on the foot rest, a fresh cup of French roast coffee sat on the Mediterranean end table. "Hey, Sissy. Come look at this," he said.

Wendy strutted into the living room. She placed her hands on her pleasingly plump hips. "What do you want, Stanley? You know I'm trying to get the house cleaned before we go to Atlanta." She wiped a wisp of blond hair that was plastered to her forehead.

"Take a break. Check this out," he said, and then read the headline: "Murderer of Senator's Son Wins Prison Murder Case." He turned the paper for her to see the picture of Bobby coming through the door of a Courtroom in Topeka, Kansas. "The jury found him not guilty because Jake came in there with the weapon and tried to stab us. I told you they would after I came back from testifying for him last week, didn't I?"

"You did. Let me see that," she said. He handed her the paper. "He's a big ole fellow, isn't he?"

"Bigger in spirit than in size, and that's big." Stan sat wondering as she read. I don't know why that idiot didn't wait to get me alone, he thought. That was the stupidest thing he could have done, come in there with two of us playing cards. He should have known Bobby wouldn't stand there and let him stab me. I reckon the alcohol just overrode his common sense and logic. I feel sorry for his family if he had one. Don't think he ever mentioned one. It was probably in the Obituaries, if he did. Wendy broke into his thoughts.

"That's great. He's a handsome rascal, too. Nicole would love to get her hands on someone like that."

"That gives me an idea."

"Watch out, now, you'll short out those two brain cells."

"Ha, ha, don't you have jokes, today."

She smiled and fluffed his hair. "You know I love you, brother."

"Do you think you could get Nicole to visit him, someday?"

"I'm sure I can. She just didn't like Terry for being the leach that he is. It didn't have as much to do with him being in prison, as it did with him always begging for money."

"Bobby is a real good man, Sissy. If it wasn't for him, I wouldn't be here. There's a lot of things I never told you about that happened in there." He picked up his cup of coffee and sipped it as he waited for her response.

"Terry told me all about you going to that man's cell to do something to him for trying to get me involved in their affairs." She smiled and handed him back the paper.

"Is that right? Can't anyone keep a secret these days?" he said, and then smiled when he saw her grinning.

"Were you really going to hurt the man to make sure he didn't get me in trouble?"

"Damn right, I was. Bobby talked me out of it or else I would have done something worse to him than what Bobby did. By the way, will you do me a favor?"

"What do you need, brother dear?"

He pulled a fifty from his tri-fold wallet. "Next time you go by the Post Office, would you mind picking up a postal money order and mailing it to him for me?"

"Wouldn't mind at all, if you don't mind me dropping him a note to thank him for what he did for you," she said, then looked away and smiled as she began pulling at a loose string on the leg of her blue-jean short-shorts.

"What's up with that? You know I don't care, but don't you think Terry will get pissed off at you if he finds out?"

Her cheeks flushed as a bright smile lit her face. "Oh, he's going to find out something else I know he doesn't want to hear." She bent down and gave him a hug.

"And just what might that be?"

"I'm following Nicole's advice. I'm dropping the loser because I am tired of supporting his dope habit. Let him chase his next fix, since that seems to be the most important thing in his life," she said. Then she turned to go back to her cleaning, stopped, turned back to face him, and then said, "I've given up hope on him ever changing. We're through."

"Is that right?"

"Yep, that's what I should have done years ago. I have no idea why I waited so long to do it, other than my sense of devotion to him as my husband," she said. Then she leaned against the door casing. "I saw what Mamma went through with Dad and never left him, so I figured I should put up with Terry and his bad habits. By the way, has she called you lately?"

"I talked to her Thursday evening. She seemed depressed about being back in jail. Maybe we can visit her tomorrow."

"She should have known not to drink again. How about Veronica? Heard from her?"

"Jasmine spoke to her last night. She's still at the prison working as a counselor, now."

"That's good. Do you think she can help Bobby?"

"In some ways, yes, but not with getting out. About the best thing she could do for him is to give him a little action. The poor guy ain't been laid in years."

"You're sick."

He grinned. "Yeah, I am. Seriously, though, if the law doesn't change or if he doesn't somehow get a break in his case, there's not a lot of hope for him getting out. It would take some new evidence, or a new Supreme Court case he could use, somehow. Congress made it really tough on prisoners by passing a bill called the Anti-terrorism Effective Death Penalty Act in 1996, after Timothy McVeigh bombed the Oklahoma City Courthouse, or whatever it was. They made tougher habeas corpus rules for federal prisoners to follow in order to have their cases reviewed once their cases are final. You know, once the normal appeal process is over."

"That doesn't seem fair."

"It's really not, but, the law is the law. The government has the guns and they do what they want to do. Anyway ...."

"Didn't you mention that he had some lawyer, with some kind of a strange name, like Zambrosha, Zadawaski, or some foreign name, like that?"

"Zachariah Zambroski, I believe. Why?"

"I saw it on CNN that some lawyer got busted yesterday for taking bribes from clients and I think that was his name."

"Hmm, if that was him, I'd be surprised if he ended up where Bobby's at. Most people like him go to the easy spots, what's called Camps."

"Do you think Bobby will ever get out?"

"It's possible, I guess. He let me read his legal work and I still question the whole ordeal with him. Something doesn't seem right. I just don't see Bobby ever harming anyone he liked. Even though they had some beer bottle they found in the car of the senator's son with Bobby's fingerprints on it, that still doesn't mean he killed the guy. But, since Bobby was in a blackout, he couldn't say what had happened. There's a girl who may know more, but he doesn't know how to locate her. Maybe we'll find out the truth one day."

"Maybe so."

"Who knows what will happen. As long as he doesn't give up fighting, and I'm sure he won't, who knows what may come up. Hell, they may even change the laws since they know the laws passed after 1984 are a failed experiment. Just as many people get out and return to prison as they did before their tough-on-crime laws got started so some politician could get a vote."

She crossed her arms and tightened her lips for a second before she spoke. "I don't reckon there's much 'Justice' for the common person, these days. Justice is something reserved for those affluent enough to afford it, or for those who come from a long line of politicians with power. That's really sad."

"That it is, but at least Mamma was one who received it when she went to court for. ... you know," he said, then looked out the window.

Wendy moved over and sat on the arm of the matching recliner Stan was sitting in. "Do you ever think about what happened?"

He stroked his mustache a few times with his right thumb and forefinger, then twisted the right tip. He glanced at her and saw her pulling at another string on her shorts. "I try not to think about it, but always do," he said. "It's like I once told Bobby, I can see it just like it happened again. Unless I'm busy doing something that keeps my mind occupied, it's always there waiting to haunt me. I've never been able to get it out of my mind for very long. How about you?"

Tears welled. She pulled a Kleenex from the box on the end table, dabbed the corner of each eye. "God knows how many times I have prayed not to think about all the blood and things that I saw that day. I was so afraid he had killed you, at first. I mean, when he turned and hit you with his elbow, and I saw how hard you hit the ground, I thought--" She stopped and cupped her face in her hands as she wept.

Stan got up and when she stood, he put his arms around her neck and pulled her close. "It's okay, Sissy," he said, as he patted her back. "We're going to be okay. You want to go see Mamma tomorrow?"

She nodded. A tear dripped on Stan's shirt. She pulled away and then forced a smile. "I'm sorry," she said, as she brushed at the makeup and mascara on the front of his shirt, above his heart. "I'll wash it for you."

He looked down to where she continued to wipe. "Don't worry about that, Sissy. It'll give Jasmine something to do. Jessica keeps her washing clothes anyway."

He hugged her again and kissed the top of her head. She grabbed him around the waist and rested her head on his chest. A moment later, she let go and looked up. "What time you want to go visit Mamma?"

"Let's go early before it gets too crowded, okay?"

"I'll meet you at the house so I can run in and kiss the baby. How does she like school?"

"Okay. She whines when I first drop her off and sometimes she doesn't want to let go of me, but when Jasmine picks her up in the evening, she says she's excited to see her and starts yapping about things that go on in class," he said, then smiled. "If I'm there when she gets home, she runs up to me and usually tells me something about her day at school. Every time she does, she's so excited she can barely get the words out, so I guess she likes it."

"That's good," she said. "Let me get back to what I was doing and then get ready to leave for the show. Fix yourself something to eat if you like. The refrigerator's full. All right?"

"I'll wait until we leave. I want to get a Blizzard at the Dairy Queen. You wouldn't believe how many times I sat in those damn prison cells and wished I could go somewhere and buy what I wanted to eat, instead of having to go to that loud-ass dining hall, or to get up and make something for myself."

"Well, you don't have to wish anymore. You're free, now. Let's put that in the past and move toward the future," she said, and then went back to work.

After they had went to an exotic car show that afternoon, he returned home and took Jasmine and Jessica out to a movie theater in Marietta to see an animated movie. Wendy stayed home and wrote Terry the Dear John letter to let him know she was filing for divorce. She called Nicole later. "Meet me at Applebee's at 7:30, if you don't have anything going on tonight. I know you're a popular lady with the men, but I would really like to see you to share some good news," she said.

"What kind of good news?"

"I'm not tellin' darling." Nicole agreed to meet her without further resistance.

When they met in the parking lot, Wendy jumped out of her new Lexus and said, "Well, I did it."

Nicole put her hands on her hips. "Did what, Love?"

"Dropped the loser."

Nicole smiled and then leaned forward to give her a hug. "It's about time, darling. Let's go in and celebrate," she said, as she let go from the hug. She grabbed Wendy by the arm and led her inside. A hostess escorted them to a table, where they sat and talked for two hours, as they ate fried shrimp and french fries. Wendy drank tea. Nicole drank a Sex on a Beach, and then they decided to leave.

Out in the parking lot, Wendy said, "Oh, I forgot to ask you what Stan wanted me to."

"What's that darling?"

"I told you about his friend, Bobby."

"Unh, huh, the big, handsome one in prison."

"Yeah, well, Stan wanted to know if you would try to visit him one day. You know, to cheer him up. He called Stan earlier today and he let me talk to him for a few minutes. He seems like a nice person."

"He's in for murder and you think he's a nice person?"

"I said he sounds like a nice person, but as far as whether he is a nice guy or not, I don't think his crime has much to do with that, since Stan questions whether Bobby is even guilty."

"I don't know, maybe he is innocent. A lot of innocent people have been freed from death row over the years, now that DNA can help prove their innocence, so--"

"He was in a blackout when the crime happened."

"Oh."

"Stan said he read some of the court documents and the evidence didn't really seem to prove that he committed the crime. There was something about a beer bottle with Bobby's fingerprints on it. It was in the car of the man who was killed. Anyway, I can have Stan to give him your phone number if you're interested."

"Honey, I don't really have a lot of time, but you can give him my number. Hell, we might even have some phone sex," she said. The corners of her mouth raised toward her eyes. "I can always find time for anything to do with a little sex." She grinned and then laughed.

Wendy smiled and grasped Nicole's arm. "You'll never change, will you, dear?"

"Hell, no. I'm having too much fun to change this late in the game."

"Well, all right then," Wendy said. "See you later on. I'll call and let you know when Stan gives him your number."

Nicole nodded as she stooped to slide into the seat of her Ford Focus. "Bye, Love," she said, as she waved goodbye.

The next morning Wendy pulled into Stan and Jasmine's driveway. By the time she turned off the engine and turned to get out of the car, Jessica was at her door. "Hey, baby," Wendy said, as she reached down and gave her a hug. "Where's your daddy?"

"In the shower. Said for you to come in."

"Well, then let's do that, okay?"

"O, kay. Let's go, Aunt Wendee," she said as she grabbed her by the hand.

Jasmine met them at the door. "Hello, stranger," she said, holding open the storm door leading into the living room.

Jessica let go of her hand and ran toward her room. "Don't run in the house, darling," Jasmine said.

"O, kay, Mommy," she said, clearing the corner.

After they had hugged, and then sat on the brown leather sofa, Jasmine said, "Stan'll be out soon. Can I get you anything, coffee? I have some good cinnamon rolls and snack cakes."

Wendy smiled, as she pulled her hair back behind her ears. "No, I'm fine. Thanks for asking."

"You doing okay?" Jasmine said. She rearranged a tiny figurine on the coffee table, before reaching for a miniature chocolate peppermint patty.

"Yeah, all is well. Things at work are about the same. Nothing's changed. I'm still working with the computers all day," she said. "Looking forward to seeing Mom today. How are things with you?"

"Sure you don't want one of these?" she said, holding out the bowl of peppermint patties.

Wendy shook her head. "Thanks anyway."

"Everything is really good. It sure is nice having Stan back home. Did he tell you he already got a raise at work?"

"Oh, yeah, he called and told me about it that night. I'm very proud of him. He'll have his own crew in no time. He always liked building things, beating on boards with a hammer, and that sort of thing," she said.

Both smiled.

"Remember, that's what he was doing when y'all met?"

Stan walked into the room drying his hair with a towel. "Did I hear you two talking about me?"

"Sure did," Wendy said. "I was bragging on you."

"Braggin' on me?"

"Yes, she was," Jasmine said. "Said you'd have your own crew before long."

"Just might do that. You ready to go?"

"I am, but it doesn't look like you are."

Jessica rushed into the room. "Daddy, daddy, look?" she said, holding a cricket between her right thumb and two of her fingers.

"What you got there, my little princess?"

"Baby bug."

"That's a cricket. Where did you get it?"

"By the back door."

"Carry it back and let it go, okay. You wouldn't want someone holding you captive, would you?"

"No," she said. "O, kay, Daddy. I'll let it go free, like they did you." Then she turned and walked away.

"That's so cute," Wendy said.

Both of them nodded, pride beaming from their eyes.

"Let me finish getting ready," Stan said. He went back to the bedroom. Five minutes later, he and Wendy were driving toward the Clayton County Detention Center.

At the jail, the door clanged open for him and her to enter the visitation area: A waxed and shined hallway leading to a row of steel doors on the left side of the hallway. The doors opened into cubicles that were divided by steel walls and Plexiglas partitions to prevent the passage of cigarettes, drugs, hacksaw blades, handcuff keys, and an assortment of other contraband items desired by prisoners who want to commit devious acts. He took a deep breath as they entered the area. The scent of a lemon/lime disinfectant assaulted his nostrils. He looked at Wendy. "I hate these places," he said.

"I do, too."

The jailer announced where each visitor must go. "Masons, door five," he said.

Inside the booth, he let Wendy sit on the round stool. A couple of minutes afterward, their mother entered on the other side, wearing a loose-fitting orange jumpsuit. Each of them smiled before she picked up the phone. Stan let Wendy speak first. "Hey Mom. How are you doing?"

Stan put his hand on the glass, his eyes moist. He smiled to cover the pain. Edna did the same. He noticed the lines around her mouth and the crow's-feet on the sides of her swollen eyes. She must have been crying, he thought.

Wendy nodded her head. "I'm okay. We were just missing you and decided to come down to see how you are doing. ... Unh huh, she's fine, said to give you her love. She's taking care of Jessica. ... Maybe she'll be able to come next time if you don't get out... I will." After a few more minutes, she said, "Here he is," and handed Stan the phone.

"Hi Mom. ... I'm doing great. How about you? ... You know I know how you feel. ... It brightens my day to see you, too, but not in here. I don't know why you started back drinking. ... I know it's tough, but you know you can't drink and get behind the wheel of a car. ... I'm sorry, Mamma. I didn't mean to upset you." He wiped his eyes. Wendy patted him on the back. "I just hate seeing you in here... Unh huh, I know."

"Ask her if she's heard any news about getting out?"

"Did you hear what she said? ... She wants to know if you heard anything about when you'll be getting out." He turned to face Wendy and held the phone against his ear. "Her Probation Officer said she may get out next week. ... She may have to go into a treatment program and then go to A.A. meetings. ... That would be good." He talked a little longer and then said, "Okay, here she is. I love you, too, Mamma." He handed Wendy the phone.

"Five minutes," the jailer yelled.

"He just said we only have five minutes left, Mamma. We'll come back again next week if you don't get out. Be sure to call and let us know what the lawyer says. ... Okay. If you need to go into the treatment program, I'll come and carry you. ... All right. ... I love you, too. She wants to say something to you real fast," she said. She handed Stan the phone.

He listened for a moment. "It's okay, I understand. ... I know you need help. ... Don't worry about it, okay? We forgive you and just want you to get some help. ... I miss you, too, Mamma. We'll come back as soon as we can if you don't get out. Be sure to call and let us know what happens. I'm going to call Mrs. McCormick to see what she can do. I need to speak with Derrick anyway. ... Okay, I will. He's yelling that our time is up. ... I love you, too. Bye," he said.

Both waved before they turned to leave the booth and began the long walk down the corridor. Stan put his arm across Wendy's shoulder when he noticed her wiping tears from her eyes. They ambled along the hallway, stopping to wait for steel doors to open and close before they reached the area to exit the building.

"Hold up right there," a guard said. "Let me see your driver's license, please."

Wendy handed them to her. After she was cleared, Stan went through the same process before they walked back to the car in silence. Once inside the car, Stan said, "Damn, I hate leaving her in that place. I never thought she'd be back inside a jail. What about you, did you think she'd start drinking again after being quit for so long?"

"Nope," she said, shaking her head. "I didn't. It shocked me. Hopefully, it will be her last time."

"I sure hope so. I damn sure don't want to see the inside of another cell again. I've had enough of the insane world of incarceration," he said. Then he put in his favorite CD of Five Finger Death Punch.

Wendy looked at him before putting the car in reverse. "Let's listen to this instead, all right?" she said and handed him the "Blown Away" CD by Carrie Underwood.

"If you insist." He frowned and ejected the other CD and put in Blown Away.

"Thanks. I bought it after I heard "Good Girl." What she sang about in it helped me make up my mind about getting a divorce from Terry."

He wrinkled his nose and cut his eyes in her direction. "Really."

"I'm serious. It made me realize I had lived under the illusion of him doing all the things he had told me he would do before we were married. But, all he did was sell me a pipe dream. He will never be the person I hoped he would be."

"I'm sure you're right on that one, Sissy. He's something else. Lucky to still be alive."

She nodded. Moments later, she played the title cut and with watery eyes, sang along with Carrie.

Stan sat listening until it was over. "Wow."

"What?"

"It made me wonder what our lives would have turned out like if a tornado had blown away Dad, instead of Mamma shooting him and having to go to jail."

She giggled. "Me, too." She opened her eyes wide, covered her mouth with her hand for a couple of seconds. "I'm sorry. I know it's not funny. I was laughing because I had thought about the same thing the first time I heard it. We're so much alike, it's strange."

"At least Mamma wouldn't have had to have gone to jail and could have been with us. That reminds me, I need to call Derrick and Mamma McCormick."

"Do you think she can help Mamma?"

"We'll find out in a flash." He opened the glove compartment and pulled out his Android cell phone and pressed the autodial button. Ten seconds later Derrick answered. Stan said, "What's going on in your neck of the woods?"

"Tell him I said hello," Wendy said.

He put the phone to her ear. "Hey, Sexy," she said. Then she smiled at his response. "Bye, darling."

"You're such a flirt," Stan said to her, as he removed the phone from her ear.

A smirk creased her lips. "I can't help it. It comes naturally." She grinned and kept her eyes on the road.

He talked with Derrick for a few minutes, who told him his Mother was at some political event. The next day, while sitting in his favorite spot out on the patio he had built, he called and spoke with her.

"Sure, I can help. I know every judge in the county and will gladly call to put in a good word for Edna. Everyone makes mistakes, don't they?" she said.

The following Thursday, the judge released their Mother. Wendy was at court with her, and after she was released, carried her to Charter Oaks for treatment. Stan was at work driving nails when his phone rang. He stopped to take the call when he saw it was Wendy. "Hey Sissy, what's up?"

He listened intently as she said, "Mamma told me to let you know she'll call as soon as they let her, and for me to be sure to tell you that she loved you, and that she promised she'd do better this time and not let us down."

He walked outside to the cooler to drink some water and to get away from the drilling, banging, and sawing sounds being made by his coworkers. "Well, I'm glad to hear that. Let's just hope she can quit again."

"I want to believe her, but. ..."

"Well. ..."

"You know I've never had a problem with the drugging and drinking. ..."

"You're the goody-two-shoes of the family."

"Cut it out. You know what I mean. It's hard for me to understand why you and her want to do the same things Daddy did, when you know how it turned out--"

"Let's not go there, all right?"

"I'm sorry. ... I don't mean anything by it. Okay?"

"Yeah, right."

"Stanley, you know how proud I am of you because of how good you've been doing since you got out. It's just hard for me not to worry that you'll go back to doing drugs and drinking like Mom did."

He sat on a pile of 2"x4"s and watched a murder of crows chase a red-tailed hawk. "Don't worry that pretty little mind of yours. I'll be okay either way. The most I'll do is smoke a joint and maybe drink a beer on special occasions--"

"That's what scares me. What if you start back and can't stop? Then what?"

"I can't see that happening. Let's forget it. I gotta get back to work."

"Well. ... okay," she said. "Oh, hold up. I forgot to tell you. Bobby called Nicole last night."

"He did?"

"She said she loved his deep voice," Wendy said. Then she laughed a moment. "You know how wild she is." She stopped and snickered a few seconds. "You won't believe what she said."

"I'll believe just about anything about her."

"She said his deep-resonating voice made her Cooter tingle when he talked." She stopped to laugh again.

He laughed hard with her for a moment. Then he said, "I guess that means he'll be calling her again, then. I don't know why he hasn't called to let me know he had talked to her."

"He might not have had enough money or phone minutes. You want me to wire him the money you gave me?"

"If you like. It must have been him that tried calling last night. I had three unidentified callers when I checked. Anyways, I gotta go now. I love you."

"Love you, too. Bye."

He hung up the phone and then went back to work. He pounded the nail heads with his 28-ounce Eastwing hammer, trying to release the frustration he felt from their conversation. He couldn't stop thinking about what she had said about him and their mother. Damn, man. She'll never forget about me going to prison or forgive me for jumping on Dad before he got shot. That really pisses me off. Hell, all I was trying to do was to protect her, he thought. I wish the hell a tornado had blown him away before he ruined our lives. Ping!

"Damn it!" he said, after the nail shot out from under the hammer head. He had almost busted his finger.

"Having a hard time over there?" a co-worker said.

"Yeah, man. It's one of those days."

"It's a better one than some of those you had in that other place, isn't it?"

He smiled. "Damn right it is. Just having to deal with my past, but at least that's what it is, the past."

"That's right. Just let it go and get on with your life. You can't change what has happened. Work on preparing yourself a future and you'll have a better past to remember."

"Thanks, man," he said. He paused pounding. He stopped and thought about Big Bobby coming into his cell and helping him get ready to go stab Jake; trying to talk him out of doing it because he didn't want him to spend the rest of his life in prison. What a friend.

"I'll be right back," he said. Then he stepped outside to call Wendy. When she picked up, he said, "If you don't mind, send him a hundred for me. I'll pay you back the other fifty when I get paid."

"Why the generosity?"

"Gratitude, Sissy," he said. "Gratitude for the life I am living now because of him."

"Okay, I'll send it in the morning," she said and hung up the phone.

He wiped the sweat from his forehead with the back of his hand, looked up at the orange-streaked sky, and then walked over to the water cooler for another drink before he went back inside. At the cooler, he wished he could sit with Bobby and talk some more about his life, remembering the day on the bleachers. Maybe one day soon we'll be able to do it again, but not in prison. God willing.

Coming Soon !

UNKNOWN INNOCENCE
by
"Mr. D."

His next novel is on the horizon. Find out how DNA and political pressure put an innocent man in prison, and how the lovely ladies of the Lonely Rooster Lounge and the Star Shadow Gentleman's Club help to free him.

About the Author

Mr. D is one of the pseudonyms used by the author in his many writings. He is a professional writer who has been published in various international magazines. He often writes inspirational essays which is why he's using a pseudonym.

His sister once told him that if she picked up a book or novel that she had bought based on his reputation established through his other writings, and then read this one, she would not read another one. (She's almost a saint and struggles with the reality of prison life which is captured in *Under Pressure*.)

www.ingramcontent.com/pod-product-compliance
Lightning Source LLC
Chambersburg PA
CBHW060621130626
46555CB00002B/606